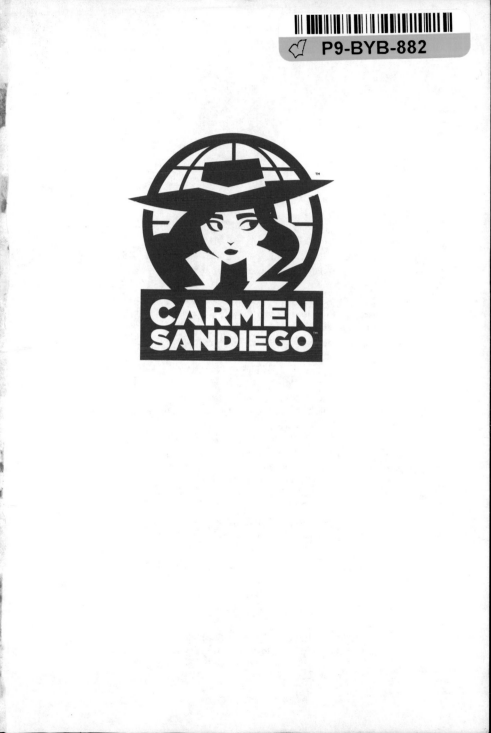

Written by Sam Nisson

hmhbooks.com

Cover artwork by Chromosphere
Background design and layout by Elaine Lee
Character design by Keiko Murayama
Character color by Linda Fong
Additional help from Sylvia Liu and Eastwood Wong
Interior artwork by Artful Doodlers
Interior design by Chrissy Kurpeski
Art direction by Rachel Newborn

The text type was set in Adobe Garamond Pro.
The display type was set in Proxima Nova and CC Biff Bam Boom.

Library of Congress Cataloging-in-Publication data is on file.

ISBN: 978-1-328-62906-7 paper over board
ISBN: 978-1-328-62907-4 paperback

Printed in the United States of America
DOC 10 9 8 7 6 5 4 3 2 1
4500772269

CARMEN SANDIEGO™

CHASE YOUR OWN CAPER

ENDANGERED OPERATION

HOUGHTON MIFFLIN HARCOURT

BOSTON NEW YORK

VILE PLOT

THE MOOD WAS GRIM in the VILE faculty lounge. The five VILE instructors, leaders of the world's most powerful criminal organization, were meeting to make their plans. Many of VILE's recent schemes had been stopped by their former-student-turned-renegade-thief, Carmen Sandiego. They were looking for ways to make up lost profits.

"I've got a dandy of an opportunity," said Coach Brunt, an enormously strong woman who spoke with a thick Texas drawl. "I am in contact with a very wealthy collector who has offered to pay a fortune for all the items on this list." She slid a piece of paper down the table for the other instructors to see.

Professor Maelstrom picked up the list. He was a stern-looking man with pale skin and a voice that could send shivers up your spine. "Amur tiger, black-footed ferret, hawksbill turtle," he read. "My dear Coach Brunt, is this a list of animals?"

"Not just any animals," Brunt answered with a grin. "Every animal on this list is extremely rare or endangered—which means they're worth a pile of money."

"Disgusting," said Countess Cleo, sticking her nose in the air. As always, she was perfectly dressed in the finest clothes and jewelry. "The only animal I'm interested in is mink."

Dr. Saira Bellum picked up the list. "There are some fascinating creatures here," she said, pushing her glasses up on her nose. "If we decide to move forward, I can arrange for their proper feeding and transportation."

Shadowsan, a master ninja who never smiled, crossed his arms over his chest. "I was not aware that VILE had become a pet store," he growled.

"Lighten up, Shadowsan," said Brunt with a smile. "A great thief can steal anything. Doesn't matter if it's got fur and claws, so long as it makes us a fortune."

"An excellent point," said Maelstrom. "I propose a vote. All in favor of this operation, raise your hands."

Brunt, Maelstrom, and Bellum raised their hands right away. More reluctantly, Cleo and Shadowsan followed. "Outstanding," said Brunt. "Now, which animal shall we capture first?"

Will VILE succeed in their plot to steal the world's rarest animals? In this story, it's up to you. Your choices will lead to one of twenty endings.

ARE YOU READY?

Turn to page **5**.

YOU ARE A ZOOKEEPER at the Schönbrunn Zoo in Vienna, Austria.

As you proudly tell visitors, Schönbrunn is the oldest zoo in the world. It was built in 1752 by Emperor Francis Stephen as a place to keep his collection of exotic birds, monkeys, and other creatures. In 1906, it was home to the first baby elephant ever born in a zoo. These days, the zoo keeps more than seven hundred kinds of animals, trying to give them all a generous habitat where they can live full lives, the way they would in the wild.

You love your job, although it's a lot of hard work—feeding the animals, watching for signs of disease or discomfort, cleaning out their living areas. Today, you are looking after the zoo's newest arrival,

Nadezhda, a baby Amur tiger. Amur tigers are the largest type of tiger in the world, living mostly in the birch forests of eastern Russia. They are also an endangered species, with only about five hundred and forty alive in the wild. Nadezhda means "hope" in Russian, because with so few Amur tigers remaining, each one carries the hope of the species.

It's late evening, and the Schönbrunn Zoo is closed to the public for the day. You let yourself into the nursery building where Nadezhda lives. Sadly, her mom wasn't paying enough attention to her, which is not uncommon for first-time tiger moms, so the veterinarians at the zoo decided that she should be fed by hand.

"Nadezhda, suppertime!" you call. She stays in a fenced-in area that takes up almost half the room, full of toys and fun places for a baby tiger to hide. Usually, she toddles out right away when she hears your voice, but today you don't see her. A pang of worry clenches your stomach.

You notice that the back door to the nursery building is open, although it should be closed and locked at this time of night. You look out to see two people fleeing around a row of trees. One of them is a large man holding something about the size of Nadezhda's carrying case.

WHAT DO YOU DO?

▷ If you go for help, turn to page **35**.

▷ If you chase the tiger thieves,
turn to page **83**.

"LET'S GO AFTER THE CROPAN'S BOA!"

you say. "That's an amazing story. They're an endangered species, one of the rarest snakes in the world. In fact, they're so rare that scientists couldn't find one alive for more than fifty years."

Carmen smiles. "And I thought *I* was sneaky. Where are they hiding?"

"They live in only one part of Brazil. A group of herpetologists—that's snake scientists—was determined to find one, so they put up posters describing the snake and asking the local people to help. Their plan worked—some workers found a Cropan's boa on a road and remembered it from the posters, so they caught it and gave it to the scientists."

"Wow," says Carmen. "If VILE is collecting rare animals, I can see why they'd want that snake. Where in Brazil does it live?"

"The Atlantic Forest," you tell her. "South of São Paulo."

"Then that's where we're going," Carmen says confidently. "Player, book us a flight for São Paulo!"

"Who's Player?" you ask.

"I'll introduce you on the plane."

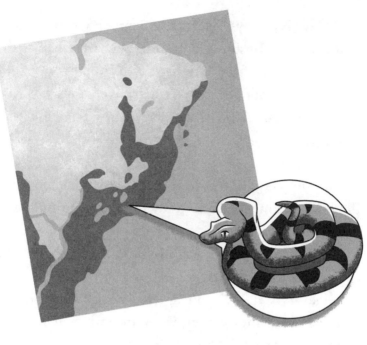

▶ ▶ ▶

Two hours later, you are taking off from Vienna
International Airport on a private jet. You can hardly
believe this is happening—you've never been outside of
Europe.

There are two other passengers, a brother and sister
named Zack and Ivy, who come from Boston, in the
United States. It turns out that Player is a teenage computer genius who lives in Niagara Falls, Canada. He's
a vital member of Carmen's crew, doing research for
missions, hacking into security systems, and arranging
transportation—all from his bedroom.

"Hey, Ivy," says Zack. "Remember when I caught that snake on Boston Common? The trick is to grab it right behind the head so it can't bite you."

"I think your memory is defective," says Ivy, playfully punching Zack in the shoulder. "That snake *did* bite you."

"Only twice!"

"Right," says Ivy. "And that one was, like, ten inches long. We definitely don't want to get bitten by a giant poisonous boa."

"Actually," says Player over a speakerphone, *"the Cropan's boa doesn't have any venom."*

"Player is right," you agree. "Boas kill using *constriction.* That means they wrap around their prey and squeeze to cut off the blood circulation."

"Yikes," says Ivy. "No hugs."

"So how do we catch it?" Zack asks.

"If you know what you're doing, it isn't actually that hard," you explain. "You can use something called a snake hook to lift the snake and guide it into a bag or bucket."

"That will be your job," Carmen tells you with a smile. "Now let's all get some sleep. We'll be in the air for a while."

You realize how tired you are after your night of adventure, and you happily discover that your seat tips all the way back until it's flat like a bed. You close your eyes and listen to the gentle hum of the engines . . .

► ► ►

You wake to Ivy shaking your shoulder. Rubbing your bleary eyes, you sit up and see sunlight streaming through the airplane windows. You look down at the coast of Brazil, with hills, farms, and patches of forest stretching into the distance.

"Our snake is down there somewhere," Carmen says.

"That's the Atlantic Forest," you explain, "one of Earth's most diverse ecosystems. It holds about twenty thousand species of plants, plus all sorts of birds, mammals, reptiles, amphibians—every kind of life. Five hundred years ago, it was bigger than Austria, Germany, and France combined.

Now, though, most of it has been cut down, which is the main reason animals like the Cropan's boa are in trouble."

"I'm no jungle expert," Zack offers as he gazes out the window, "but that place still looks pretty big. I mean, how are we supposed to find one snake?"

"Yeah," says Ivy, "especially a snake that's been hiding for fifty years."

You think for a moment, and then you have an idea. "After the scientists spent some time with the Cropan's boa, they released her back into the forest. They implanted her with a small radio transmitter so that they could track her movements and learn more about the species."

"Interesting," says Carmen. "So we could track that radio transmitter too. Player, can you hack into it?"

"It's not like a cellphone," says Player. *"We would need to build a tracker and then get close to pick up the radio signal."*

"I could build the tracker, no problem, with the right supplies," Ivy offers.

"That sounds good," says Player. *"But what if VILE also knows about the snake's radio transmitter? They do have a head start."*

"Good point," says Carmen. "So here's the plan. Zack and Ivy, you go into São Paulo and pick up the supplies you need to build the tracker. I'll head straight for the forest where the boa was released and scout for VILE."

"What about me?" you ask.

"Your call."

WHAT DO YOU DO?

▷ If you scout ahead with Carmen, turn to page **97**.

▷ If you stick with Zack and Ivy, turn to page **57**.

"WAIT!" YOU SAY, holding up your hands. "Nadezhda—the tiger cub—she's crying because it's past her suppertime and she hasn't had anything to eat."

"I gave her a bottle," says Moose Boy, "but she wasn't hungry."

"She'll eat only if she feels safe. And no offense, but she doesn't feel safe with you because she doesn't know you."

Tigress sneers. "What's your point?"

"Please," you say, "take me with you. I'll take care of Nadezhda, and I promise I won't be any trouble."

"Sounds like a good idea," says Moose Boy.

"Coming from you, Moose Boy, that means absolutely nothing." Tigress rolls her eyes. "But fine. And while you're at it, you can show us the way to the west entrance."

You decide to play along for now. At the very least, you'll be able to make sure that Nadezhda is well taken care of. And you'll keep your eyes open for any chance to escape.

Moose Boy picks up the carrying case, and the three of you continue along the path. Nadezhda crouches down on her blanket and growls. You smile at her, hoping that a friendly face will give her some comfort.

"How long?" Tigress demands.

"Not far now," you tell her. You take them on a long, circular path that leads around the aviary, a forested area surrounded by a net, where the zoo keeps its flying birds. You see the west entrance ahead, a ticket booth, and a row of turnstiles behind a locked gate.

Tigress makes a phone call. "Our ride will be here any minute," she says. Using one of her claws, she picks the lock on the gate, which swings open with a squeak. You exit onto the city sidewalk outside the zoo just as a black van pulls up to the curb. A small, sharp-faced man wearing glasses looks out from the driver's seat.

"Hello, Otter Man," says Tigress.

"Good to see you as always, Tigress. I trust that cage contains our feline prisoner."

"Another successful mission," she says.

"*Ja,* very good. Moose, load the kidnapped cub into the back of the van. Tigress, you are to report in for your next assignment —"

Suddenly, flashlights flicker over the van from inside the zoo. "Hello!" a voice calls. "Who opened this gate? You know you can't park there!"

"Guards!" Otter Man cries in alarm. "We can't let them follow us!"

"You take care of the cub," Tigress tells him. "I'll take care of the guards."

Otter Man nods. This would be the perfect time for you to get away while everyone is distracted! But you'd have to leave Nadezhda behind . . .

WHAT DO YOU DO?

▷ If you make a run for it,
turn to page **75**.

▷ If you stay with Nadezhda and
the thieves, turn to page **123**.

YOU HOLD YOUR BREATH and charge through the drifting smoke, reaching down to grab the satchel with the egg. You slip for a moment in the grass but then find your feet and sprint toward the door of the ranger's hut.

You feel a sharp pain in the back of your neck, and when you put your hand on the spot, you pull out a tiny dart. Lady Dokuso is smiling, her parasol aimed directly at you. Your legs feel like rubber as the whole world goes sideways . . .

When you wake up, you are in the cabin of the heli-jet, lying on a bench that is bolted to one of the walls. Across the cabin, Carmen is lying on a similar bench, looking like a crumpled heap of red. The three VILE guards have been propped up against the back wall, their heads drooping, still unconscious.

At the front of the room, Lady Dokuso sits with her back to you, punching buttons on the jet's flight computer, dark sky outside the windshield in front of her. You feel the gentle hum of the engines and realize that you are flying.

A monitor above the computer pops on, showing a large woman with a friendly smile on her face. "Howdy,

Lady D," the woman says. "I gather the mission was a success?" You recognize the voice—Coach Brunt.

Lady Dokuso smiles faintly. "More successful than we could have possibly hoped," she says. "I captured the kakapo . . . along with even more valuable prey." She gestures toward the back of the cabin, where Carmen is lying unconscious.

Brunt's eyes go wide with wonder. "Is that . . . ?"

"Carmen Sandiego," Lady Dokuso boasts. "I know that she has been a great deal of trouble for some of your newer graduates, but she presented little challenge to an experienced operative such as myself."

Brunt claps her hands eagerly. "This is a glorious

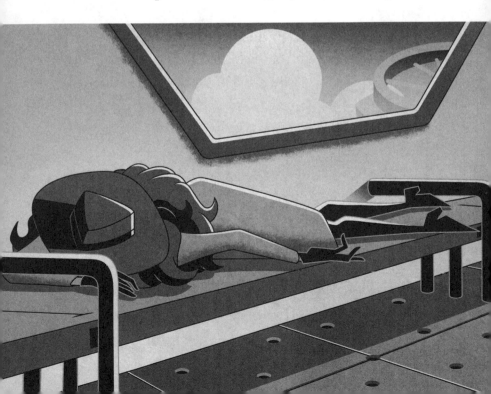

day," she declares. "You can skip the zoo and bring her directly back to Vile Island. I can't wait to begin her . . . *reeducation.* Fine work, Lady D. This will not be forgotten." The screen goes black.

You're not going to let them take Carmen Sandiego! You try to leap to your feet . . . but the poison in your system still has you mostly paralyzed, so instead you just roll off the bench and flop on the floor with a thud.

Lady Dokuso turns around and raises an eyebrow. "Ah, it appears that our zookeeper needs another sip of sleep juice." She aims her parasol and shoots a poison dart into your leg. The world goes black again.

THE END

YOU WALK TOWARD THE TABLE where
Le Chèvre is sitting until you are standing close behind
him. Over his shoulder, you can see the screen of his
tablet. He is watching videos of people from around the
world doing parkour tricks.

As quietly as you can, you reach out and take the
tracker from the bench. In Le Chèvre's video, someone
narrates in Japanese while a woman effortlessly bounds
up the side of a building. "Not so great," Le Chèvre
mutters scornfully.

Quickly and quietly, you walk away, clutching the
snake tracker. You're out of the restaurant now. Which
way should you go? You decide to walk toward the village center and look for a place to hide until you can
meet up with Carmen. The world's greatest thief should
be impressed that you swiped the tracker from right
under VILE's nose.

Between two buildings, you spot a high fence around
an empty yard and decide to hide there. But just as you
open the gate, you see El Topo, the other VILE operative, walking toward you.

He sees you, too, and sees that you are carrying the
snake tracker. "Stop!" he shouts.

Moving quickly, you dodge through the gate and

slam it shut, dropping a crossbar in place to lock it from the inside. El Topo kicks from the other side, but the fence is strong and topped with barbed wire, so you should be safe for now.

You still need a place to hide. Looking around, you see that you are in a wide, cluttered yard, with piles of plywood, a tractor that looks like it's being repaired, and stacks of wooden crates. You try a door that leads into one of the buildings, but it's locked.

Suddenly, the dirt in the middle of the yard puckers up into a mound, as if something is pushing from below. A moment later, El Topo comes bursting out in an explosion of dirt, launching himself from the ground. Somehow, he dug a tunnel under the fence! You are so surprised, you stumble backwards and fall.

"I think we can both agree," he says, "you have been caught. So please, hand over that device you have stolen. It is more important than you know."

"I know what it does," you say, holding the tracker in front of you. "And I think snakes belong in the forest."

With all your strength, you hurl the tracker at a wall. It smashes open and lands on the ground with an electric buzz.

El Topo shakes his head sadly. "I wish you had not done that," he says.

Suddenly, you hear a fierce barking, and a moment later, three wild-looking dogs charge out from behind the nearest building. The front dog is the size of a German shepherd, with pointy ears, matted fur, and vicious teeth. It leaps up on El Topo, knocking him to the ground.

El Topo swings out with his fist, swatting the dog

backwards. A second dog gets its teeth around El Topo's wrist. The third runs circles around him, barking wildly.

You steady your breathing and consider the three canines. They don't look like trained attack dogs, more likely local animals protecting their turf. El Topo may not know any better, but fighting back is the worst thing he could do.

"Hey!" you shout, waving your hands in front of you to show that you are no threat. The first dog turns away from El Topo and stalks toward you, growling viciously. You hold out your hand. The dog sniffs it and then starts barking furiously while the other two dogs circle around you.

"We're in their territory," you tell El Topo. "They're just trying to show us they're in charge. Get up and walk slowly toward the gate."

El Topo stands. The two of you walk toward the gate in the fence, showing your hands and never turning your backs on the three dogs. They bound around you, barking and snapping near your legs, but they don't bite. You open the gate and slip back out onto the road, closing the gate behind you.

El Topo wipes his forehead with the back of his hand. He looks pale, and you can see that he is genuinely shaken. "Thank you," he says. "I thought those dogs would be the end of El Topo."

"They were just being dogs," you say.

"I am sorry," says El Topo. "Although I am grateful for what you have done, I cannot let you go after you have ruined our mission."

El Topo grabs your arm just as Le Chèvre comes running up. You are trapped. The two men take you in their pickup truck to the port town of Itajaí, where they put you on a boat. You are locked in a windowless cabin for days.

When your cabin door finally opens, you stagger up on deck, weary and seasick, blinking in the bright midday sun. You see that the boat has docked on a tropical beach, with a large gray building looming out of the forest nearby.

An enormous woman stands at the end of the dock, her hands on her hips, watching you with a smile. "Welcome to VILE Academy," she says.

"I don't understand . . ."

"My name is Coach Brunt," she says, "and I've had my eye on you. You showed gumption when you took on Tigress. You showed thieving skill when you swiped the tracker from Le Chèvre. And the way you handled those dogs, well, that was grade A prime. Sugar, I think you might be VILE material."

"Whaaat?"

"VILE. It stands for Valuable Imports, Lavish Exports. We are the world's greatest organization of thieves, stealing for fun and profit. Every year, we recruit forty students to train here at VILE Academy. How would you like to be one of them?"

"Do I have a choice?" you ask.

"Well, of course you have a choice, sugar. We don't want anyone at VILE Academy who doesn't believe one hundred percent in our mission."

WHAT DO YOU SAY?

▷ "Yes"—turn to page **55**.

▷ "No"—turn to page **139**.

"LET'S BACKTRACK to the other bridge," you say.

"Good vote," says Ivy. "I knew I liked you."

"Aww man," says Zack as he turns the car around. "You guys are no fun!"

It's frustrating to lose time while Carmen is waiting, but a couple of hours later, you reach the second bridge and are back on track. By late afternoon, you arrive at your meeting spot at the intersection of two roads, near where the Cropan's boa was found.

You find Carmen sitting on a fallen tree trunk, waiting for you. She opens the back door of the car and slides in next to Ivy.

"Sorry we're late," Zack says. "*Ivy* wanted to take the long way."

"No problem," Carmen replies. "I've been looking around, but no sign of VILE yet. Hopefully we got here first. Ivy, how's that tracker working?"

"Let's find out," Ivy says. She proudly holds up a chaotic tangle of parts and wires, with an antenna sticking out the top. She flips a switch and then adjusts a knob back and forth until the tracker starts to beep. "Bingo!" she says.

"What's the beeping mean?" Zack asks.

"It means we're in the snake's general neighborhood," Ivy explains. "Remember, the snake has a radio transmitter under its skin, right? This tracker beeps when it picks up the signal. The stronger the signal, the faster it beeps."

Carmen nods her understanding. "So it's like a game of hot and cold. If the tracker beeps faster, we're getting closer."

"Sounds like fun," Zack declares. "You guys ready to head into the woods for some snake hunting?"

"We could," says Carmen. "Or we could wait for VILE to find the snake first, and then use the tracker to follow *them*."

WHAT DO YOU THINK?

▷ If you want to follow the snake's signal now, turn to page **60**.

▷ If you want to hide and wait for VILE, turn to page **112**.

YOU SLIP THE DEVICE into your ear. It fits perfectly, so small that you doubt anyone will notice you're wearing it.

"Hi there," says a friendly voice in your ear. It sounds like a teenage boy. When you don't say anything, he says, *"You can talk. The earpiece has a microphone built in, so I can hear everything you say."*

"Who are you?"

"I'm Player. You're the zookeeper from Vienna, right?"

"Yes, that's me."

"Okay, listen, I know this is weird, but my friends and I are trying to get all those animals back to their homes, and we're hoping you can help. Does that sound okay to you?"

"Wait . . . who are you again?"

"I'm Player."

"I know; you said that, but *who are you?* And who are your friends? And *where* are you?"

"Look behind your ship about twenty degrees to starboard. Do you see a blinking light?" Sure enough, when you look out over the black ocean behind the cargo ship, you see a distant light flash one, two, three times.

"I see it," you say.

"That's our boat," says Player. *"The problem is, the*

ship you're on is faster than ours. So we need you to put your ship into reverse for a minute to give us time to catch up. Can you get to the bridge?"

You look up toward the bridge, a brightly lit room at the back of the ship, with stairs leading up to it. "I see it," you say, "but the captain is inside."

"I'm not sure how to help you with that," Player admits.

Figuring you'll decide what to do once you get there, you climb the metal stairs that lead up to the bridge. The door at the top is unlocked, and you walk in to see a jumble of controls and displays. Two separate radar readouts on green and black screens show the ocean around you.

The captain sits in a worn chair, reading a magazine. "What?" he asks flatly without even looking up.

"Otter Man sent me. He says to stop the ship. We . . . we need to pick up one more animal, and another ship is meeting us at sea."

"Hmph," the captain snorts, setting his magazine aside. "The little tiger was supposed to be the last one, and then full steam ahead for Greece."

"I don't know. I guess there was a change of plans." When the captain still looks skeptical, you add, "The order comes straight from Coach Brunt."

That gets his attention. "Fine," he says. He consults a large compass hanging over his control station and then pulls two levers all the way back. You can feel a change in the hum of the ship beneath your feet as the powerful engines go into reverse, slowing the ship down.

Three seconds later, you see Otter Man come up from a stairwell at the far end of the deck, sprinting toward the bridge. He must have felt the change in the ship's direction and is coming to find out why. The captain has gone back to his reading and hasn't seen Otter Man yet, but you don't have much time . . .

WHAT DO YOU DO?

▷ If you tell Otter Man a lie,
turn to page **107**.

▷ If you lock the door to the bridge,
turn to page **44**.

YOU KNOW THAT OCEAN CURRENTS

can be powerful and unpredictable, so you better get out of the water as soon as possible. You wave your arms frantically as you bob up and down. "Over here!" you shout. "OVER HERE!"

At first, you're not sure if they spotted you, but then you see that Zack is wheeling his boat around and coming back toward you. The second Interpol speedboat sees you too and races toward you from the opposite direction.

You climb a sharp point of rock that sticks out from the ocean, holding tight against the crashing waves. Zack reaches you a second before the Interpol speedboat, and you leap from your perch into the back of his boat. Ivy and Carmen do their best to catch you, and the three of you tumble in a heap onto the deck.

Zack swerves just before he collides with the Interpol speedboat, so close that the sides of the two boats scrape and bounce off each other. The impact sends the Interpol boat crashing into the rock that you jumped from. It flips end-over-end into the air, the driver tumbling into the ocean as Zack speeds away.

"You did it, bro!" Ivy whoops.

"Just like our street-racing days, only wetter!" Zack cheers.

And then you notice a thrumming sound and see an Interpol helicopter coming toward you. "Turn off your engine immediately!" booms a voice from above. "You are all under arrest." The helicopter turns so that it is flying directly above you, matching your speed and direction.

"Oh boy," says Zack. "I don't think I can outrun a chopper."

"I'll take care of this one," says Carmen. She points her arm toward the sky, and a grappling hook shoots  out of her sleeve, attaching to the helicopter's landing gear. Incredibly, Carmen flips up into the sky and catches hold of the helicopter. A moment later, the pilot tumbles out and lands with a splash in the ocean.

"Whoa!" says Zack. "I hope she knows how to fly that thing."

"Carm can do pretty much anything," says Ivy as the helicopter bobs in the air and then flies toward land. "Now let's get out of here before they send a submarine after us."

As you zoom toward the mainland, you see the Interpol cruiser up ahead, trying to cut you off. "Don't worry," Zack says as he adjusts your course. "We're a lot faster than that thing."

"WAIT!" Chase's voice booms from the cruiser. "Carmen Sandiego dropped something!" He waves Carmen's red fedora in the air. "I know how much she is attached to her special hat, and I wish to return it to her . . . as a gesture of goodwill."

Chase flings the fedora out over the water. It spins through the air and then drifts down onto the ocean like a falling leaf. Zack steers past it, reaching down to scoop it from the water. "That was nice of him!"

"Yeah, real nice," says Ivy, grabbing the hat from her

brother. "I'd say there's a zero percent chance he didn't put a tracker in this thing." She feels under the brim of the hat and pulls out a thin disk of metal. "Bingo."

Ivy flips a tiny switch on the tracker. "There, I turned it off." She hands the tracker to you. "Here you go. You can keep it as a souvenir."

"Thanks," you say, examining it front and back. It's about the size of a postage stamp, with visible circuits running through it and a tiny black switch on one side. "Are you positive they can't follow this?"

"Not unless you turn it back on," Ivy says.

"So don't turn it on," Zack adds helpfully.

WHAT DO YOU DO?

▷ If you throw the tracker in the water,
turn to page **121**.

▷ If you slip it into your pocket,
turn to page **71**.

YOU SPRINT OUT THE FRONT DOOR

of the tiger nursery, looking around for a guard. You pull out your phone and dial the number for the police, holding the phone to your ear as you run past the hippopotamus pool and toward the center of the zoo.

"Stop!" a voice calls out behind you.

You wheel around to see a young woman in a red trench coat standing right in the middle of the path. She wears a wide-brimmed red fedora on her head that casts a shadow over her face. "Please," she says, "hang up the phone."

Something in her voice makes you want to trust her, so you touch the button to end your call. "Who are you," you ask, "and what are you doing here?"

"My name is Carmen Sandiego," she says. "I'll tell you everything, but right now I need to move quickly, and I need your help. I know that something has been stolen here tonight, but I don't know what. Can you tell me?"

"A tiger," you say. "An Amur tiger cub. Her name is Nadezhda."

Carmen nods. For just a moment, you wonder if she's the one who took Nadezhda, but then she pulls

up the brim of her fedora and you see the warmth and genuine concern in her eyes. "Okay," she says, her voice full of reassuring confidence. "Where's the nearest exit from this zoo?"

"Wait," you say. "I don't understand. Who would steal a baby tiger?"

"The most dangerous criminals in the world," says Carmen. "And they have a head start. Will you help me catch them?"

WHAT DO YOU SAY?

▷ "Of course I'll help!"—
turn to page **67**.

▷ "Well . . . I'm just a zookeeper."—
turn to page **95**.

"LET'S GO FOR THE KAKAPO!" you say.
"They're a kind of parrot, the largest parrots on Earth, and one of the most endangered birds."

"Okay," says Carmen. "If you wanted to steal one, where would you go?"

"They used to live all over New Zealand, but now they're only on a few small islands."

Carmen nods. "Player," she says, "we need a flight to New Zealand."

"Who's Player?" you ask.

"I'll introduce you on the plane."

▶ ▶ ▶

Two hours later, you are taking off from Vienna International Airport on a private jet. You can hardly believe this is happening—you've never been outside of Europe.

There are two other passengers, a brother and sister named Zack and Ivy, who come from Boston, in the United States. It turns out that Player is a teenage computer genius who lives in Niagara Falls, Canada. He's a vital member of Carmen's crew, doing research for

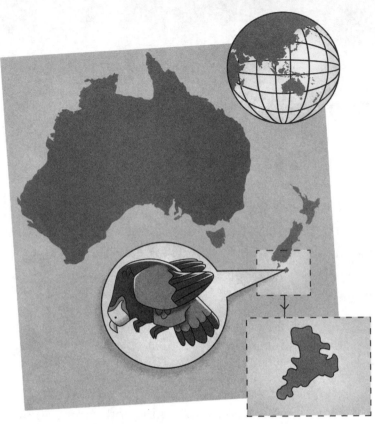

missions, hacking into security systems, and arranging transportation—all from his bedroom.

You sit next to Carmen, looking at her laptop. She pulls up a picture of a kakapo standing on a log in the forest. It looks like an extra-large, extra-chubby parrot, with moss-green feathers and a wise face.

"Aw," coos Ivy, "it really is cute."

"That kakapo should get up in the trees," Zack suggests, "where it won't be so easy to catch."

"That's the problem," you explain. "Kakapos can't fly. For thousands of years, they lived on islands that had no predators on the ground, so they were safe walking around. Then, about seven hundred years ago, Polynesians came to New Zealand and brought predators like dogs and rats. Later on, Europeans brought even more predators. The kakapo became an easy meal."

"Predators are the worst!" Zack complains.

"It's not the predators' fault," you say. "Every ecosystem on the planet is a delicate balance. There are dozens of examples of humans bringing plants or animals to a new place and causing problems."

Ivy frowns. "Sounds like humans are the worst."

"Not all humans," you explain. "An amazing team of scientists and rangers have been working to save the kakapos from extinction."

"That's right!" Player chimes in from the speaker-phone. An image of New Zealand pops up on Carmen's screen and then zooms in on three small islands. *"Scientists got rid of all the predators on these three islands, so the kakapos have a place where they can live safely, just like they did a thousand years ago."*

"Okay," says Carmen, "sounds like VILE will be headed for one of those islands. Which one?"

You point to one of the islands on the map, near the southern coast. "Let's start with Codfish Island, right here," you say. "That one has the most kakapos."

Carmen nods. "In the meantime, let's all get some sleep."

You realize how tired you are after your night of adventure, and you happily discover that your seat tips all the way back until it's flat like a bed. You close your eyes and listen to the gentle hum of the engines . . .

▶ ▶ ▶

When you wake up, you are descending into Invercargill, a coastal city in southern New Zealand. *"I've already arranged for a boat,"* Player says over the speakerphone. *"Once you land, it's a short trip by sea to Codfish Island."*

Ivy looks concerned. "We don't usually do our capers right in the middle of the day," she says. "Shouldn't we wait until after dark?"

"Did you hear the part about them not flying?" Zack argues. "We can't give VILE all day to catch one."

Carmen looks uncertain. "What do you think?" she asks you.

WHAT DO YOU THINK?

▷ If you want to go to Codfish Island right away, turn to page **78**.

▷ If you want to wait until night, turn to page **101**.

YOU SHUT THE METAL DOOR to the bridge and turn the lock. The captain looks up from his magazine. "What in the world are you doing?" he asks.

"Just locking the door," you say. "You can never be too safe, right?"

He rolls his chair back and stands. "We're in the middle of the Adriatic Sea, twenty miles from shore. I'd say we're pretty safe."

"What's going on?" Player asks in your ear.

At that moment, Otter Man arrives at the bridge. He rattles the handle as he tries to open the locked door. "Hey!" he shouts. "Why is this door locked? Why are we slowing down? Let me in immediately!"

The captain fixes you with a scowl and walks toward the door, but you step in front of him, blocking his path. "Wait," you say. "Please listen to me. All the animals on your ship—they've all been stolen, taken from their homes. These people are criminals!"

The captain laughs. "Of course they're criminals. Who else carries a boatload of endangered species halfway around the world? That's why I'm charging them ten times my usual rate. Now, MOVE."

Grudgingly, you step aside. The captain unlocks the door to the bridge and swings it open. *Now or never*—you rush him from behind, pushing him in the back with both your hands. He stumbles forward, colliding with Otter Man, and you slam and lock the door so that they are both stuck outside.

"Hey!" shouts the captain.

Otter Man pounds on the door with his fists. "THIS IS MUTINY!" he hollers. "Let me inside!" He kicks the door with all his strength, but the lock is too strong. He pulls out his phone and screams into it. "MOOSE! I need you on the bridge. MOOSE BOY!"

"Player," you say, "are you close? I don't have much time."

"Getting closer," says Player. *"Your ship is slowing down. Just keep those engines in reverse for another minute . . ."*

"I don't think I have a minute." You gulp. The glass window of the bridge overlooks the entire deck, and you see Moose Boy already galloping up the stairs. Otter Man points wildly at the door, and the big man nods, backs up, and charges with his shoulder down. The whole room

shakes as the door bends inward. Moose Boy backs up
for another charge, and **CRASH**—the door comes flying off its hinges as he bounds into the room.

"Throw the zookeeper overboard," says Otter Man
coldly, "while I get this ship moving again."

Moose Boy grabs you. You kick and struggle as he
drags you down the stairs, but he's impossibly strong.

"I'm sorry about this," he says. "But you know how it goes." He pulls you toward the railing at the edge of the ship's deck, and you see the white crests of churning waves forty feet below. Moose Boy lifts you by the back of your shirt—

CLANG. Something flies out of the darkness and attaches to a metal crate behind you. You see that it's a grappling hook attached to a zipline. A moment later, a young woman comes flying along the zipline, then drops and lands on top of the large crate that holds the black rhino.

You gasp, looking at this woman who appeared out of the sky. She's wearing a red hat and a red trench coat, which whips around in the ocean breeze.

Otter Man comes sprinting across the deck. "Stop her, Moose!" he hollers. "That's CARMEN SANDIEGO!"

Moose Boy drops you and charges toward the large crate where Carmen has landed, jumping and catching the top of the crate with his massively strong arms. Just as he pulls himself up, Carmen leaps over his head, somersaulting through the air and landing gracefully behind him on the deck.

She smiles at you. "Thanks for slowing down the ship."

"No problem," you say.

Moose Boy leaps back down from the crate with an angry roar. He picks up a thick metal pipe, which he

48

holds like a club as he strides toward Carmen. "You've got nowhere to run, red lady," he booms. "And I'm a lot bigger than you."

"True," says Carmen, "but *he's* a lot bigger than *you.*" She points behind Moose Boy, who glances over his shoulder just in time to see the black rhino charging toward him. Carmen must have unlatched the door to its cage!

The rhino thunders across the deck. Moose Boy hurls himself to the side—just in time to avoid the rhino's horn—and right over the railing of the ship.

You hear a splash from the dark ocean below as the rhino slows down and starts padding around the deck. Otter Man yells, "Moose, NO!" and then steps toward Carmen with his fists clenched.

"Listen," Carmen says to him. "Neither one of us wants your friend to drown. So here's the deal. We let you take the lifeboat to go save your friend. You let us take this ship."

Otter Man scowls but nods his agreement.

An hour later, Moose Boy and Otter Man are gone. You were able to soothe the black rhino by feeding it apples and carrots and have led it back into its cage.

Carmen has spoken to the crew: She will pay their fee; they will return all the animals to their homes. Two of Carmen's friends have come on board from the other ship as well, a brother-and-sister team from Boston, in the United States. You're surprised to learn, though, that Player isn't with them but has been talking to you this whole time from his bedroom in Niagara Falls, Canada.

You are sitting on the stairs, holding Nadezhda in your arms as the sun rises over the eastern horizon. Carmen Sandiego walks over and sits down next to you.

"She's cute," Carmen says.

"Yeah," you answer. "I won't be able to hold her this way for much longer. It's hard to remember sometimes that she's going to be a two-hundred-and-fifty-pound apex predator soon."

"Well, until then, she's lucky to have you."

You smile. "Carmen," you say, "I don't know how to thank you for saving us."

Carmen shrugs. "You don't have to thank me. It's what I do."

THE END

"NO WAY!" you tell her.

The woman leans her face closer to the screen, staring at you with a terrifying scowl. "I tried being nice," she says. "Now I'm going to crush you like a—"

You pull the video device off the dashboard and toss it out the window of the truck.

You drive west, deeper inland, into Brazil. There is forest all around you, good habitat for the Cropan's boa, but you want to make sure to drive far enough that VILE will have no chance of ever finding her again, even with a tracker.

As the sun starts to rise, you pull the truck over to the side of the road and hoist the bucket down from the back. You pry off the lid and pull out the heavy sack that holds the snake, placing it at the edge of the forest and loosening the drawstring at the top.

A couple of minutes later, a triangle-shaped head pokes out from the top of the sack. The boa flicks her tongue a few times, smelling the breeze, understanding her new surroundings. She slithers forward, extending to her full length as she stretches toward the forest.

She stops at the base of a tree and raises her head, like she's looking at you with one black pebble eye. You are struck by how beautiful she is, more than five feet long, with a yellowish body and a black diamond pattern along her back.

The snake climbs the tree, coiling her body around and sliding up the trunk in a way that seems to defy gravity. Although you feel a bit silly, you wave goodbye. You hope that Carmen can rescue all the stolen animals, but even if she can't, you are proud that you have rescued this one.

In a few seconds, the Cropan's boa disappears into the canopy of leaves overhead.

THE END

YOU TURN AND RUN back down the path the same way you came.

"Get back here!" Tigress shouts from behind you. You glance over your shoulder to see her streaking toward you incredibly fast. She swipes at you as you turn a corner, her razor-sharp claws slicing holes in the back of your shirt.

The sea lion habitat is straight ahead, and you sprint toward it, looking for a way to shake Tigress. Desperately, you put a hand on the fence that surrounds the sea lion pool and vault right over, falling ten feet into the water.

The sea lions are asleep at this time of night, so you have the pool to yourself. You start swimming to a rocky outcropping where the sea lions sun themselves during the day. There's a splash behind you—it seems that Tigress isn't afraid of getting wet.

As you pull yourself, dripping, up onto the rocks, you look around for some escape. You spot an enormous hose hanging from the stone wall, which the zookeepers use to wash the habitat. You pull it down as Tigress climbs out of the water behind you, hair drenched and matted to her head, snarling with fury.

"I already sounded the alarm," you lie. "The police will be here any minute."

"Is that so?" she sneers. "Then I guess I better deal with you quickly." She stalks toward you, ten claw-tipped fingers ready to strike. *Are those claws part of her costume,* you wonder, *or part of her?*

Moving quickly, you twist the metal handle that controls the enormous hose. You feel the water surge through and point it toward Tigress, blasting her with a stream that sends her hurtling back into the pool. As Tigress shrieks in frustration, you run for a ladder that leads out of the sea lion habitat.

You climb the ladder quickly, looking over your shoulder to see Tigress climbing back out of the pool to chase you. When you're almost at the top, powerful hands reach down and lift you onto the path. It's Moose Boy. You kick against the railing to try to break free, but his grip is so powerful that he barely notices.

"What are you going to do with me?" you plead.

Tigress stands at the bottom of the ladder, wiping water out of her eyes. "The people we work for have a little rule," she says. "No witnesses."

THE END

"YES," YOU SAY. "I'll do it!"

Coach Brunt gives you a thunderous clap on the back. "I had a good feeling about you," she says merrily. "Welcome to VILE Academy."

A few weeks later, classes begin. You meet the recruits who will be your classmates: petty thieves, white-collar grifters, and others who have shown a talent for crime. You take classes from five criminal masterminds, learning important skills like self-defense, pickpocketing, and forgery. You make friends with the other students.

Coach Brunt seems to favor you, and one day she gives you a gift: an English mastiff, one of the largest and most loyal breeds of dog. You name him Brutus and train him to fetch things for you, to sniff out valuables, and to attack on command. Some of the other students are jealous, but Brunt insists that Brutus is much more than a pet.

A few weeks later, Brunt gives you a second gift, a falcon

chick that you raise by hand. You name her Betty, teaching her to deliver small packages and to wear a camera around her neck for airborne spying.

After months of training, you pass your final exams and graduate to become a VILE operative. You plan to take Brutus and Betty out into the field to give you an edge on every mission.

You even pick the perfect VILE code name: the Zookeeper.

THE END

"I'LL STICK WITH ZACK AND IVY," you say.

As the jet approaches São Paulo, you see an enormous metropolis sprawled beneath you. Player tells you that São Paulo is Brazil's largest and richest city, with more people than any other city in the Southern Hemisphere. It's also a tremendous center of industry and one of the fastest-growing cities in the world.

After you land, Carmen hires a smaller propeller plane to carry her out over the forest where the boa lives. You, Zack, and Ivy rent a car and drive out into town.

While Ivy shops for electronics, you pick up some supplies to help catch the Cropan's boa: a snake hook, a large plastic bucket, and plenty of insect repellent. Zack meanwhile buys hot dogs from an outdoor stand. When he brings them back to the car, you are surprised to see that they are topped with corn and peas and have mashed potatoes lining the bun.

Zack just shrugs. "Different countries like different stuff on their hot dogs," he explains, "but in my experience, they are *all* delicious." He takes a bite and nods enthusiastically. You take a bite and agree—delicious!

Zack hops into the driver's seat of the rental car, and you head out of town—he's the official driver for Carmen's crew. You ride up front so that Ivy can use the whole back seat as her workshop. She's busily attaching different parts with screws and wires, although it's hard to see yet what the tracker will look like when it's done.

After a few hours on the highway, you turn onto an unpaved side road, following a map toward the spot where you're supposed to meet Carmen. On either side, the forest seems eager to reclaim the road, with branches sticking in front of your car and vines creeping out over the dirt. Your car bounces and lurches.

"Stop bumping, bro," Ivy complains. "It's like a roller coaster back here. You're knocking my screws loose."

"You do your job and I'll do mine," Zack answers irritably. "Anyway, have you seen this road? It's not exactly the interstate."

You come to a place where the road crosses a river called the Rio Juquiá, but a sign says that the bridge is closed for repairs and suggests a detour. Zack moans in frustration, then gets out of the car and walks out across the bridge. It's shaped like an arch, made of concrete, with supports that go down into the river. Only the middle section is missing, maybe a five-foot gap. He gets back in the car and slams the door confidently.

"I can jump it," he says.

"We're not going to jump it," says Ivy. "Let me see the map. Look—there's another way across down here."

"That's, like, two hours out of our way! Come on, Ivy, you know Carmen is waiting for us. I'm going to jump it, and that's final."

"You're not going to jump it, and *that's* final."

"Which one of us knows more about driving?"

"Which one of us knows more about not being a knucklehead?"

Zack crosses his arms across his chest in annoyance. "Looks like we're gonna need a tiebreaker." They both look to you.

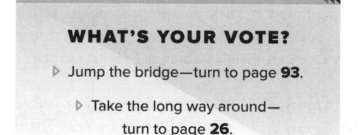

WHAT'S YOUR VOTE?

▷ Jump the bridge—turn to page **93**.

▷ Take the long way around— turn to page **26**.

"LET'S GO AFTER THE SNAKE NOW,"

you say. "I don't want to risk VILE catching her."

"Okay," Carmen agrees. "We can catch her and move her before VILE ever has a chance."

Zack drives back and forth along the road while you all listen carefully to the beeping of Ivy's tracker. When you reach the point where the beeping is fastest, Zack stops the car and pulls over to the side, halfway into the forest.

"We're on foot from here," you say.

The forest is thick, the ground choked with low-lying bushes, the spaces between the trees crisscrossed with vines. "Is there anything dangerous in there?" Ivy asks.

"This is jaguar habitat," you reply, "but you could spend years in the forest and never see one. The most dangerous animals are the mosquitoes, which can carry some serious diseases, so everyone bug-spray up."

Zack stays in the car to keep a lookout and be ready for a quick getaway. You, Carmen, and Ivy spray on bug repellent and then push into the forest. You move slowly, wading through the tangle of plant life. Every fifty feet or so, Ivy holds the tracker in the air and you all listen for whether the beeping is getting faster or slower.

The air under the trees is hot and feels heavy on your skin. Bugs swirl around your heads, and creeping plants catch and scratch your legs with every step. Sometimes it feels like you're going in circles trying to follow the beeps. You're getting irritable.

Finally, you find the spot where the beeping is the fastest. Ivy brushes aside wide fern leaves around your feet, looking for the Cropan's boa. "What would it look like?" she asks.

"About six feet long, yellow and black with a diamond pattern on its back." You look up into the dense canopy of leaves above your head. "But I don't think it's on the ground. The Cropan's boa is a great tree climber, which might be why they're so rarely seen."

"So you're saying she's right over our heads?" Carmen asks.

"Probably."

"Okay," says Carmen. "You're our expert snake catcher. You think you can get up there?"

Honestly, you aren't sure. You look at the sunlight flickering through the leaves overhead, and it looks like a long way up. Luckily, there are vines everywhere, coiling around the tree trunks and hanging from overhead, which can help you climb.

Time to climb. You brace your foot against a knot in a tree trunk and reach for a vine above your head. Pulling yourself up, you get to the lowest branch in the tree and swing yourself up so that you are sitting on top of it. There are vines everywhere, and you're able to climb hand-over-hand, higher and higher, until the leaves are so thick that you can see only a few feet in any direction.

There's no sign of a snake, so you keep climbing. All around, you hear the buzzing of insects and the chirping of birds, like the forest is pulsing with life. Finally, your head pops out from the top of the canopy and you see treetops all around you, like a giant green field.

The Cropan's boa is in the very next tree—the snake so rare that only a few people in the world have ever seen one. She's coiled in and out of branches like a complicated knot, her tail dangling, her head up. Although she is motionless, you know that she is watching you with her glassy eye.

Steadying yourself, you reach into your backpack and pull out your snake hook, which you extend to its full length. It's a simple tool, basically a pole with a hook at the end that you can use to catch the boa. It feels wrong to take her from her treetop perch, but you tell yourself that it's for her own good.

Something in the distance catches your eye, something leaping from tree to tree. You try to remember what kind of monkeys live in the Atlantic Forest, but it looks too big to be a monkey. As it gets closer, you realize it's a person, leaping through the trees with impossible skill, like a cartoon Tarzan.

One final leap, and he lands on a treetop next to you, swinging around and then perching in the highest branches. You see that he is a tall, wiry man with a beard. Attached to his waist are a snake hook like yours and an electronic device with an antenna—another snake tracker.

"I do not know who you are," the man says in a French accent, "but I suggest that you leave. This snake and I have plans, and you are not invited."

You realize that he's a VILE operative, sent to catch the Cropan's boa. You hold up your snake hook like a weapon, hanging on to the tree with your other hand. "You're not taking the snake," you say firmly.

"You should not challenge Le Chèvre to a fight in the treetops," the man scoffs. Leaping effortlessly from his perch, he swings his snake hook at you. You block his blow like a sword fighter as he hops onto another tree.

Suddenly, the Cropan's boa springs into motion. With surprising grace, she extends to her full length and slithers along her tree branch, disappearing into the canopy.

Grunting his annoyance that the snake has escaped, Le Chèvre swings at you again with his snake hook. You latch your own hook onto his and yank, pulling him off balance. He tumbles, dragging you with him, and you both fall, crashing through vines, branches, and leaves.

You hit the ground hard, twisting your arm the wrong way. A few feet above you, Le Chèvre catches a vine and swings himself easily onto the forest floor, where Carmen and Ivy are waiting.

"Carmen Sandiego," Le Chèvre sneers, "how is it

possible that you are always everywhere you should not be?"

"Stealing snakes now?" Carmen fires back. "Why don't you pick on someone your own species?"

Le Chèvre jumps, swings on a vine, somersaults in the air, and lands on a thick tree branch fifteen feet up. "No man or beast can match me for climbing," he boasts, holding up his snake tracker. "And I can follow that snake anywhere it goes."

Carmen raises her arm, and a grappling hook shoots out from the sleeve of her trench coat, knocking the tracker out of Le Chèvre's hand and smashing it against a tree trunk. "How are you going to follow the snake now?" she quips.

"Argh!" Le Chèvre hollers. "How can one person be so much trouble? I will be back." With that, he leaps higher into the treetops and is gone.

"What now?" you ask. As you sit up, you feel a stabbing pain in your wrist, worse than anything you have ever felt. Glancing nervously at your arm, you see that it's bent the wrong way.

"Now we're going to take you to a hospital to get that arm taken care of," Carmen says. "It will take some time for VILE to make a new snake tracker, and when they do, we'll be waiting for them."

Ten minutes later, you are sitting in the back seat

of the car, cradling your throbbing arm, driving back toward São Paulo. "Thank you," Carmen says. "We would never have gotten this far without you."

You are proud of everything you have done but sad that your part in the story is over.

THE END

"OF COURSE I'LL HELP!" you say. "I don't know where they went, but if they're trying to escape quickly, they probably headed for the west entrance."

"Got it," says Carmen. "Lead the way."

You sprint through the zoo, with Carmen Sandiego right behind you. You race past the large, rocky habitat where the grownup Amur tigers live, making a sharp left turn through a food court to reach the aviary. Luckily, you know these paths like your own backyard, so it's no problem finding your way in the dark.

The aviary is filled with trees and covered in a high netting so the zoo's birds can live with room to fly. "Hold on!" you say. "I know a shortcut." Using your keys, you open a gate in the fence that surrounds the aviary so that you can cut through the middle rather than go all the way around.

Inside, the aviary is kept wild and feels like being

in a forest, with trees swaying and birds calling overhead. You dash through and open a gate on the far side, arriving at the edge of the zoo, steps away from the west entrance.

Carmen puts a hand on your shoulder. "There!" she says, pointing.

On the other side of a fence that surrounds the zoo, you see a black van, parked on a city street with the motor running. Someone is in the driver's seat, but you are too far to see their face in the dim light. As you watch, the van begins to pull away. "Wait here," says Carmen. "I'm going after them."

She points her arm up in the air, and a grappling hook shoots out of her sleeve with a *ZZZIP,* attaching to a streetlight overhead. A moment later, Carmen hurtles upward like she's flying, landing gracefully on the sidewalk on the other side of the fence. The van pulls away and Carmen sprints after it, disappearing down the street.

So you wait.

A few minutes later, you hear a voice coming toward you along the path that runs around the edge of the zoo. You dodge behind a row of bushes and crouch low, trying not to breathe too loudly.

A young woman walks toward you, wearing what

looks like a tiger costume, a black suit with orange stripes and a pointy mask. She's talking to someone on a video screen that she has strapped to her wrist.

"Tigress, please tell me you bagged that critter," says a voice from the videophone with a deep Texas drawl.

"We ran into a little trouble with the guards, but I took care of it," says the woman in the tiger suit, whose name, it seems, *is actually Tigress.*

"Good work," says the voice on the videophone.

"What now, Coach Brunt?" Tigress asks, looking at a piece of paper. "Should I head for the next location on the list?"

"No need, kitten. We've got other operatives on the way. You've done your part, so come on back to home base for your next assignment. Brunt out!"

Tigress is now standing right next to the row of bushes where you are hiding, only a few feet away from you. She looks toward the dark zoo and holds her hands in the air like she's addressing a crowd. "Jungle animals," she says, "bow down to your queen!"

Laughing at her own joke, she turns

and walks away down the path. In a few seconds, she'll be gone.

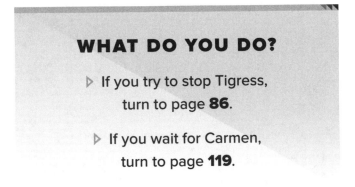

WHAT DO YOU DO?

▷ If you try to stop Tigress,
turn to page **86**.

▷ If you wait for Carmen,
turn to page **119**.

YOU SLIP THE TRACKER into your pocket as Zack speeds away.

Within a few hours, the three of you have docked at a marina on the mainland. You hear from Player that Carmen managed to land the helicopter and will meet you there soon. Zack and Ivy have gone into a diner to get some takeout while you sit on a bench outside, watching boats come and go.

You are holding on to Carmen's red fedora until you can return it to her. You try it on your head and find that it fits well. *So this is what it feels like to be the world's greatest thief,* you think with a smile.

Suddenly, a green van screeches to a stop on the street in front of you, and the back door flies open. You glimpse a woman in a kimono aiming her parasol at you—and then you feel a sting in your neck. You touch the spot and pull out a tiny dart as the world goes fuzzy. The last thing you hear before you lose consciousness is someone saying, "That's not Carmen Sandiego!"

When you come to, you are lying on a tangle of vines next to a hollow tree trunk. Where in the world are you? Looking around, you realize that you are inside an animal enclosure like the kind you have in a zoo, with a mesh wire fence on all sides.

Outside the enclosure, you see the woman in the kimono, the one who kidnapped you, talking to a much larger woman. "Good job getting the kakapo, Lady D," the large woman says. "But why did you bring back that zookeeper?"

"I apologize, Coach Brunt. We thought we were capturing Carmen Sandiego."

Coach Brunt peers in at you. "A minor mistake in an otherwise out-standing mission," she says. "We'll get this cleaned up in no time."

When the two women leave, you try to get out of the enclosure, but you can't break the fence, and the gate is locked from the outside. You start to feel hopeless—but then you have an idea. Reaching into your pocket, you flip the switch, turning on the Interpol tracker. Hoping that someone gets the signal, you sit down on a fallen branch to wait.

A few hours later, you hear helicopters overhead. Coach Brunt sprints past the cage where you are being held. "WE'VE BEEN FOUND!" she hollers. "All VILE staff, get out now!"

An Interpol officer appears outside your cage and snaps the lock on the door with wire cutters. "Who are you, and what are you doing in there?" she asks. You tell her that you are a prisoner of VILE, so she directs you to the harbor, where Interpol boats are waiting.

When you come out of your cage, you find that you are on a path through a small zoo. You pass a water tank on your right, with what looks like a rare hawksbill turtle swimming inside. On your left, you see a fenced-in area where a black rhino grazes peacefully. This must be where all the stolen animals are being held!

Leaving the zoo, you come over a ridge to see a harbor where several Interpol boats are anchored. Inspector Chase Devineaux stands by the shore, the same one who was chasing you in New Zealand. A dark-haired woman in large round glasses stands next to him, checking items on a clipboard. "Giant panda, check. Black rhino, check. Amur tiger, check. It seems that every rare animal that has gone missing is right here on this island."

Chase holds up a finger imperiously. "You are incorrect as usual, Miss Argent. For where, I ask you, is the rarest creature of them all? *Where is Carmen Sandiego?* She is the mastermind behind this entire operation."

Julia bites her pen thoughtfully. "You may

be right, Inspector. And yet it does not fit Carmen Sandiego's usual patterns to kidnap animals for a private zoo."

"Do you forget? It was the tracking device that I cleverly placed in Miss Sandiego's hat that led us to this island. How do you explain that, Miss Argent?"

"I suppose I cannot. Still . . ."

As weeks go by, Interpol makes sure that the animals are returned to their homes. The story is big news, how an eccentric billionaire stole the rarest animals from around the world to keep in his own private zoo. You notice that there is never any mention of VILE—they must be good at covering their tracks—or of Carmen Sandiego.

You return to your life working at the Schönbrunn Zoo, deeply proud of the part that you played in rescuing the animals. Best of all, Nadezhda is returned to her nursery, where she is growing into a fine young tiger.

THE END

OF COURSE YOU CARE about Nadezhda, but you're not ready to risk your life with these dangerous criminals. While Tigress and Otter Man are watching the guards, and Moose Boy is loading the carrying case into the van, you slowly take a few steps away from them . . . then a few more steps . . . and then you break into a run.

"Get back here!" Tigress snaps.

"Forget the zookeeper," says Otter Man. "We need to get out of here, *now*."

You sprint away down the sidewalk, green trees of the zoo to your right, fancy apartment buildings to your left. As you run, you imagine Tigress slashing her razor claws at your back, but after a few blocks, you are sure that no one is chasing you. You stop to catch your breath. What now?

You walk around the zoo to another entrance. Two police cars are parked out front, their lights flashing. You realize that they must know about the robbery.

As the only eyewitness to the crime, you are interviewed several times, telling your story again and again. Finally, by midnight, you are exhausted, wanting only to go home and put this terrible night behind you. As you leave, though, you are called for one final interview. You are led into an office in the zoo's administration building, where you find yourself sitting across a table from a tall, squared-jawed man in a brown suit.

"Good evening," the man says in a thick French accent. "I am Inspector Chase Devineaux of Interpol. I trust you will not mind if I ask you a few questions."

"Go ahead," you say.

"I understand that you saw the thieves firsthand, *oui?*"

"Yes, that's right."

"Very well," he says. "It so happens that I have been tracking a series of similar crimes across Europe and throughout the world. All by the same master criminal." He smacks a blurry photograph down on the table, showing a woman in a red coat half hidden in a doorway. "Carmen Sandiego!" he declares. "The crimson ghost. She was tonight's mysterious thief, *oui?*"

"No, actually," you answer. "I didn't see anyone like that."

Chase leans in so close that you can feel his breath on your face. "Are you certain?"

"Yes. Like I told the police, it was three people.

There was one girl with claws who called herself Tigress, then this huge guy named Moose Boy, then another guy named Otter Man, who met us later."

Inspector Devineaux leaps to his feet and slams both hands against the table. "Am I to understand it is your story that three people *named after animals* broke into and *robbed a zoo?* Why do you waste my time with such nonsense?"

"I . . . you asked to talk to me—"

"The witness is clearly delusional! This interview is over!" Chase waves his hand in the air and storms out of the room.

The next day, the Schönbrunn Zoo opens as usual and things return mostly to normal, although everyone is sad about the loss of Nadezhda. The police are never able to recover the lost cub, and as you imagine her growing up, you hope she is having a good life and that someone is taking good care of her.

THE END

"I THINK WE SHOULD GO NOW," you say. "If those creeps get away with another endangered animal, I won't be able to forgive myself."

Carmen agrees. And so, as soon as you land in Invercargill, you pick up your boat. It's a powerful eighteen-foot motorboat, open on top, with seats in back and front. Zack clearly loves driving it, jumping over waves as you cruise out of the harbor and into the open water.

"This is my kind of driving!" he whoops. "Nothing to hit out here."

You head across a broad channel of water called the Foveaux Strait toward a large, mountainous island dotted with trees. "Is that Codfish Island?" Zack asks.

"No," you tell him. "That's Stewart Island, which is much bigger. Take us around the north side, and we'll see Codfish Island."

Sure enough, about an hour later, a smaller island comes into view. It looks wild, with green hills that rise sharply out of the ocean. On one side, you see a sandy beach, but no houses or other signs of human civilization.

As you get closer, you see another boat motoring away from Codfish Island. "Uh-oh," says Ivy. "Do you think VILE is already getting away with a kakapo?"

"I don't think so," Carmen replies. "Look! They're coming our way."

Sure enough, the boat has changed direction and is now headed toward you. As it gets closer, you see that it has the logo of the New Zealand Department of Conservation. A man and a woman are on board, both dressed in ranger uniforms. They pull their boat close to yours and stop the motor.

"Ahoy!" the woman shouts. "Where are you headed?"

"Codfish Island," you tell her.

"Sorry," the man says. "The island is off-limits to visitors. It's a protected kakapo habitat."

"We're here to protect the kakapos!" Zack blurts. "Someone is trying to steal one of those enormous parrots!"

The two rangers look at each other with concern.

"Yeah," the woman says. "We actually got a warning from Interpol to watch out for poachers . . . but what would you four know about that?"

"Nothing," says Carmen. "Sorry for the trouble."

Carmen tells Zack to head back toward the mainland, so he turns the boat in a wide circle away from Codfish Island. Looking over your shoulder, you see one of the rangers talking to someone on his boat radio.

"Let's get out of sight," Carmen says, "and then we'll figure out what to do next."

As you sail back around Stewart Island, a cruiser appears from behind a rocky point. It's much larger than your boat, with the Interpol insignia on the hull. "This is bad," Carmen says. "The rangers must have thought we were suspicious and called Interpol."

"I see you, Carmen Sandiego," booms a voice on a loudspeaker from the cruiser, with a heavy French accent.

"This is Inspector Chase Devineaux. In the name of Interpol, I demand that you surrender immediately."

"Zack, you think we can outrun that thing?" Carmen asks.

"That big tub? No problem."

Two small speedboats zip out from behind the Interpol cruiser. They look sleek and fast as they streak to either side, tossing up ribbons of water behind them.

"Now, that's a problem," Zack says.

Zack throws the throttle on your motorboat all the way forward and makes a sharp turn back toward mainland New Zealand. You're going so fast that Carmen's red fedora flies off her head, landing in the ocean.

"Stop them!" Chase bellows as the two speedboats turn toward you. You are sitting in the front of the boat, clinging desperately as you bounce over each wave, water spraying all around you. Despite your speed, the Interpol boats are getting closer.

Zack spots an area up ahead where dozens of rocky points stick out of the ocean like teeth. "No way they can make it through there!" he shouts.

"And we can?" Ivy asks.

Zack races into the rocky area, the Interpol speedboats following less than fifty feet behind. He weaves left and right, expertly dodging the rocks. You are amazed at his driving skill, but looking down into the water, you see other rocks close beneath the surface and worry that Zack will hit something he can't see.

Zack speeds through a narrow space between two rocky teeth, with inches to spare on either side. The lead Interpol speedboat tries to follow, but one of the rocks catches its side, sending it into a spinning flip. "Yeah!" Ivy cheers. "One down, one to go!"

And then **BOOM!**—your boat hits a rock hidden beneath the surface, and the front flies up wildly. You are hurled ten feet into the air, landing clear of the boat in the foaming water. You go under for a moment and then bob to the surface, your friends already a hundred feet away.

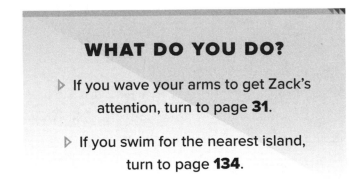

WHAT DO YOU DO?

▷ If you wave your arms to get Zack's attention, turn to page **31**.

▷ If you swim for the nearest island, turn to page **134**.

YOU SLIP OUT THE DOOR, following the two people who may have taken Nadezhda. You look down a tree-lined path that leads toward the sea lion habitat just in time to see them turn the next corner.

You chase after them. The zoo is empty of people at night and the paths are mostly dark, but you hear the comforting chatter of orangutans from an enclosure to your right. The sea lion habitat is at an intersection where three paths come together, but you don't see the thieves in any direction. Are you too late?

Something catches your eye down one of the paths: an orange plastic ball stuck halfway in the bushes. You pick it up, and it jingles with bells inside—Nadezhda's favorite toy. Now you know she came this way. You start to run, wishing your shoes made less noise as they smack against the pavement.

You turn a corner around the Elephant Park—and then you see them. About fifty feet ahead are two people, backs turned to you, huddling over an official zoo map. One of them is an enormous man dressed in a fur-hooded parka. The other is a young woman wearing what looks like a tiger costume.

They've put Nadezhda's carrying case down on the ground, a metal cage with a blanket on the bottom for her to sleep on. The baby tiger stares out at you through the wire bars, her eyes big and scared. You hold a finger up to your lips. *Shhh.*

"This stupid map doesn't make any sense," complains the woman in the tiger costume. "Straight past the orangutans, left at the sea lions, and we should be at the west entrance."

The large man shrugs. "Don't look at me," he says. "Remember, fighting is my job. Figuring things out is your job."

"Fighting and figuring things out are *both* my jobs," she snaps. "Your job is carrying stuff. Now, give me some room so I can think."

Nadezhda meows—a long, vibrating sound full of sadness and fear. The woman in the tiger costume turns around. "Stop that whining," she says to Nadezhda. "You're an embarrassment to all tigers—"

And then she sees you.

"Moose Boy," she says, "I think we have company."

"Oh hello," Moose Boy says to you. "I'm Moose Boy, and this is Tigress. Maybe you could help us out here. We're looking for the west entrance, but we've been going in circles."

Tigress rolls her eyes. "I think what my muscle-brained friend means to say is, you're about to be cat

food!" She opens her hand dramatically to show claws like daggers at the ends of her fingers. *Uh-oh.*

WHAT DO YOU DO?

▷ If you talk your way out of it, turn to page **14**.

▷ If you run, turn to page **52**.

YOU STEP OUT of the bushes. "Hey!" you say to Tigress as she walks past. "I know you took my tiger cub, and I want her back. Now."

Tigress turns around slowly and looks you up and down. She holds out her hand as if she's examining her nails—long and sharp, like actual cat claws! You realize that this person really is dangerous and wonder if you've made a mistake by challenging her.

"*Tsk, tsk,*" says Tigress, walking toward you menacingly. "Don't you know that tigers have *nasty* tempers?"

Moving faster than anyone you've ever seen, she somersaults toward you. She lands on all fours and then sweeps out her leg, tripping you onto the pavement.

"Stay down, zookeeper," Tigress taunts. She stands over you, her hands on her hips, a cruel smirk on her face, and then wheels around to walk away.

"You're never going to see your precious *widdle* baby tiger again."

You watch from the ground, rage bubbling in your chest. *No,* you think, *I'm not letting you get away that easily.* Although you've never been in a fight in your life, you leap to your feet and charge Tigress from behind, wrapping your arms around her and tackling her into the bushes. She shrieks in surprise as you both hit the ground.

As you roll through the dirt, Tigress pushes away from you and leaps to her feet. *She really is like a cat,* you think. She flashes all ten claws, the points glinting in the streetlight like daggers.

"I know you probably don't care," you say, "but Nadezhda is an Amur tiger, an endangered species!"

"The only endangered species here is you," Tigress sneers. She puts one clawed hand around your neck and draws the other back to strike. *This could be the end . . .*

"No need to be catty," says a voice from behind Tigress. Carmen Sandiego stands on the other side of the path, leaning against the lamppost like she doesn't have a care in the world. "Now, get your claws off the zookeeper."

Tigress releases you and turns to face her new enemy. "Carmen Sandiego," she growls, "how many times do I have to beat you?"

"At least once."

The two stand face-to-face, about ten feet apart. Tigress opens and closes her hands, her body tense, as if getting ready to pounce. Carmen watches her carefully, and you have the sense that these two have a long history together.

But then Tigress turns away. "You're not worth it," she says. "And anyway, you're too late. Your precious kitty cub is long gone." And with that, Tigress sprints away into the darkness.

"Are you going to chase her?" you ask.

"No point," says Carmen. "She won't tell us anything, and unfortunately she's right, for once. I couldn't catch up with the van, which means that Nadezhda is gone for now. But don't give up. My friends and I have a few tricks of our own—"

"Wait . . . What's that?" you interrupt. You spot a piece of paper lying in the bushes. Did Tigress drop it during the fight? You snatch it up and see that it's some sort of checklist:

- ☑ *Hawksbill turtle*
- ☑ *Black-footed ferret*
- ☐ *Cropan's boa*
- ☑ *Amur tiger*
- ☑ *Black rhino*
- ☑ *Bonobo*
- ☐ *Kakapo*
- ☑ *Gooty tarantula*
- ☑ *Komodo dragon*

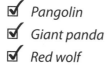 *Pangolin*

☑ *Giant panda*

☑ *Red wolf*

"It's a list of animals," you say, showing it to Carmen.

"What's a *pangolin?*" Carmen asks.

"It's sort of like an armored anteater. When they're threatened, they roll up into a ball, and their scales are so tough that a lion couldn't bite through them. It's sad, though—pangolins have been hunted so much that they're in danger of going extinct."

"That's awful."

"Actually," you say as it dawns on you, "all the animals on this list are rare, and most of them are endangered! Like the black-footed ferret—they live in North American grasslands, with fewer than four hundred left in the wild."

"VILE must be collecting rare animals," says Carmen thoughtfully, "just another treasure to steal. I'm not going to let that happen."

"Can you stop them?"

"Maybe we'll stop them together. I'm going to need someone with your expertise to help chase down all these animals. Will you come with me?"

You nod. After everything that's happened, you know you want to help in any way you can.

"Look," Carmen continues, "there are only two

animals on the list that haven't been checked off: the Cropan's boa and the kakapo. The only question is, which one should we go after first?"

WHICH ONE?

▷ The Cropan's boa—
turn to page **8**.

▷ The kakapo—turn to page **39**.

"THANK YOU," you tell Carmen. "Thank you, but no. I love my old job, and a lot of animals depend on me."

Carmen smiles. "You're a good person," she says. "The animals are lucky to have you."

The helijet is an amazing vehicle, able to travel at supersonic speeds and then land anywhere without needing a runway. You reach Austria before dawn, and Carmen drops you in Lainzer Tiergarten, a large wildlife preserve on the edge of Vienna. You hug goodbye and then walk down the steps from the helijet, waving as it lifts off into the morning sky.

That same afternoon, you are back at work at the Schönbrunn Zoo, walking through the gates surrounded by a familiar crowd of tourists and families. You check the board that shows everyone's assignments and find that your first job for the day is cleaning out the orangutan habitat—not exactly glamorous work. For a moment you wonder if you should have chosen a thrilling life with Carmen instead, but as you watch the happy faces of visiting children, you know you did the right thing.

A few days later, you see on the news that Interpol has busted an illegal zoo with a dozen rare animals from around the world. It seems that the zoo was built on a private island off the coast of Greece. You watch an interview with the officer in charge, whose name is Inspector Chase Devineaux.

"I have been tracking these animals for months," he explains. "And then I received an anonymous tip to investigate a remote island in the Mediterranean Sea. Let this be a warning to all criminals: Nowhere in the world is safe from Chase Devineaux!"

The billionaire who owns the island is arrested and the stolen animals are returned to their homes, including Nadezhda. At first, she seems unsettled by her adventure, but within a few days, she is her usual self, hiding and playing and learning how to be a tiger.

THE END

"LET'S JUMP IT," you say.

Zack pumps his fist in the air. "All right, let's do this!" He backs the car up about fifty feet, lines up with the bridge, and guns the engine a few times.

Now that the decision is made, Ivy is supportive. "You got this, bro!"

The tires squeal as Zack punches the gas and the car leaps forward. You careen over the uneven road, picking up speed, the engine roaring . . . and then your stomach lurches as the wheels leave the concrete and you are in the air. A moment later, you come down on the far side with a gut-wrenching crunch.

The car fishtails sideways as Zack furiously turns the wheel, trying to keep control. You spin one way,

then the other, and then crash into a tree. An airbag pops out of the dashboard into your face.

"WOOOOOOOOO!" Zack hollers. "HOW SWEET WAS THAT?"

"Not that sweet!" Ivy says, getting out. "Look at our car!"

You get out too and see that the front bumper is crumpled against the trunk of the tree. Smoke pours from under the hood, and one wheel is twisted into the air, spinning on a bent axle.

"But you can fix it, right, sis?" Zack asks nervously.

"Sure, I can fix it—in a garage, with all my tools and a couple thousand dollars of new parts." She sits by the side of the road and crosses her arms in fury.

Player arranges for someone to come pick you up and drive you back to São Paulo, but by the time you get a new car and meet up with Carmen, Ivy's tracker can't find any signal from the snake. You assume that VILE got there first and that the Cropan's boa is long gone.

THE END

"WELL," YOU SAY, "I'm just a zookeeper. Of course I want to get Nadezhda back, but I can't get involved with dangerous criminals."

"I understand," says Carmen, sounding disappointed. "Just tell me where they went."

"The fastest way out would be the west entrance," you say. "If they're looking at a map, that's where they would have gone."

"Got it," says Carmen, and then, "Player, can you direct me to the west entrance?"

"Who are you talking to?" you ask.

"Never mind," says Carmen, dashing off down the path.

For a moment you stand dumbstruck in the middle of the dark zoo. But then you remember Nadezhda and again dial the police on your phone. "Hello," you say, "I'd like to report a robbery at the Schönbrunn Zoo." When the woman on the other end asks what was stolen, you tell her that it was a baby tiger. At first she sounds skeptical, but then she says that she'll send someone right away.

Five minutes later, you hear sirens and you meet the police as they enter the zoo. When they ask you what happened, you tell them every detail you remember . . . except you don't say anything about Carmen Sandiego, the mysterious woman in red. You have a feeling that she'd rather be kept a secret, and that she might be your best chance of getting Nadezhda back.

As the days and weeks pass, though, Nadezhda doesn't come back. The police say the investigation is ongoing, but they never seem to make real progress, and you fear that the trail has gone cold. You also read about thefts of other rare animals around the world: a black rhino airlifted out of Nairobi National Park in Kenya, a bonobo snatched from the Twycross Zoo in England. Is it a pattern, or just a coincidence? You suppose you will never know.

And you never see Carmen Sandiego again.

THE END

YOU TELL CARMEN, "I'll stick with you."

After you land in São Paulo, you and Carmen take off again, this time in a small propeller plane. A local pilot sits up front at the controls while you and Carmen ride in the back seat, with barely enough room for the two of you. The windows are wide open, and you stick your head out to watch the ground rolling past beneath you.

You are heading toward the area where the Cropan's boa was found, flying low enough to see cars on the road and tractors in the field. You pass over a river, which your pilot tells you is the Rio Juquiá.

"What are we looking for?" the pilot asks.

"I'm not sure," Carmen admits. "Let's get as low as we can and try to spot anything suspicious."

"Going down," the pilot says, bringing the plane into a dive until you are only about five hundred feet above the ground. You circle around the area once and then twice. The forest has a thick canopy like a green carpet, so you can't see anything beneath the treetops.

Carmen notices a small dirt road that leads deeper into the forest and asks the pilot to follow it. You notice two parked motorcycles but can't see any people.

"Do you think those motorcycles belong to VILE?" you ask.

Carmen shrugs. "It could be. If VILE is tracking the snake, it makes sense that they would park out here and explore the jungle on foot. I'm going to take a closer look."

"It's not safe to fly any lower," the pilot warns.

"Not a problem," Carmen replies. "Is there any place that you can land near here?" The pilot replies that there's a runway outside a nearby village. Carmen asks him to land the plane there and tells you she will meet you soon.

"Where are you going?" you ask.

"I told you," she replies with a smile, "for a closer look." She opens the door to the airplane and steps out as casually as if it were a parked car. You look down to see her falling toward the green forest, and then a red triangle appears—somehow, she has popped open a hang glider. She soars down toward the road, landing about a hundred feet from the parked motorcycles.

"Your friend is . . . unusual," the pilot says.

Fifteen minutes later, the plane lands on a rough airstrip, little more than a dirt road through a field on the edge of a village. A handful of small planes are parked on the grass. There is a small restaurant nearby, a wooden building with tables outside, and you decide to get something to drink while you wait for Carmen.

As you sit outside, sipping a fresh pineapple juice, you notice two men at a nearby table who don't look like locals. One of them is tall, with a neatly trimmed beard and an irritated look on his face. He is holding an electronic device with a spiral antenna coming out the top, twisting a dial.

"Still nothing!" the man complains, speaking in a French accent. "This device is clearly defective."

100

"Do not despair, Le Chèvre," says the other man, who is shorter and thickly built, with spiky hair and a friendly face. "The snake must still be far away. Let us enjoy our lunch, and then we are back into the jungle."

In a flash, you realize that the device is a snake tracker, just like the one Ivy is building, and so the two men must be VILE operatives! You wish Carmen were here.

"While we have a few minutes, I think I will stretch my legs," the shorter man says. He gets up and walks off down a road that leads through the center of the village. The tall man puts his tracker down on the bench next to him and starts tapping away on a tablet.

You might be able to grab the snake tracker without him noticing.

WHAT DO YOU DO?

▷ If you swipe the tracker,
turn to page **20**.

▷ If you wait and watch,
turn to page **109**.

"LET'S WAIT UNTIL NIGHT," you say. "The kakapo habitat is protected, so we can't just walk in."

"Okay," Carmen agrees. "We'll sneak in by boat after dark."

You land in Invercargill with some extra time, so Zack suggests you stop for meat pies, a local favorite food. You enjoy a delicious cupcake-size pie full of minced meat, gravy, mushrooms, onions, and cheese, and then pick up your motorboat, which is about eighteen feet long, with seats for passengers in the front and back.

Zack drives the boat—this seems to be his job with Carmen's crew—while you ride up front on the bow. You have plenty of time before nightfall, so you cruise along the coast, watching the lush green land go by. You feel like you're on vacation with excellent new friends.

As the sun goes down, you turn toward open water. Codfish Island is about thirty miles offshore, next to the much larger Stewart Island. The ocean feels different at night, almost spooky, with endless black in every direction. As you bob along the waves, you finally see the silhouette of Codfish Island ahead. Carmen asks Zack to get close, keeping the engine low to make as little noise as possible.

You find an inlet, protected from the waves, where you can jump from the boat to the rocks along the shore. Carmen lays out the plan: You and she will explore the island while Zack and Ivy stay with the boat, ready to make a fast escape.

As you scramble up the rocks onto Codfish Island, you find yourself in a low forest. The moon is almost full, so you can see a bit where you're going. A path leads inland, which you and Carmen follow, pushing branches and brambles out of your way.

"*Psst,*" says Carmen. "Look at this!" Standing about ten feet back into the woods is a tall, box-shaped cage with an open door. "Do you think VILE set a trap?"

"Maybe," you say, "but more likely that was set by the rangers. Every single kakapo gets caught about once a year for a quick checkup. It's like going to your yearly doctor's appointment."

As you keep moving through the forest, you hear a strange sound off the path to your left, like a low trumpet blast. Stepping as lightly as you can, you move in that direction. You push into a small clearing to see one of the most delightful things you have ever seen.

Standing on the forest floor, a large bird stares up at you, its black eyes twinkling in the moonlight. It shifts from foot to foot as it considers you. A kakapo.

"What's it doing?" Carmen whispers.

"Probably out foraging for plants to eat. Kakapos are nocturnal, so this is their most active time."

Suddenly the kakapo dashes away, fluttering its wings, and disappears into the undergrowth. Carmen laughs. "They're faster than they look."

"Yeah," you agree. "Maybe it won't be so easy for VILE to catch one."

"Seriously, imagine for a minute that you were trying to steal a kakapo," Carmen wonders aloud. "What would you do?"

"I don't know. They're not easy to find. We're lucky we saw one. I mean, there are only about a hundred and fifty in the whole world, even though this has been a good year for kakapo eggs . . ."

And then you realize how you would steal a kakapo.

"That's it!" you say. "Sometimes if a kakapo lays more eggs than she can take care of, the rangers take one or two of them away to raise by hand. And this year, there were a lot of kakapo eggs!"

Carmen nods her understanding. "So the rangers probably took some away. Why steal a bird when you can steal an egg?" She checks in with Player and learns that there is a ranger's hut on the island, less than half a mile from where you are now. That's where the eggs would be kept. You start jogging in that direction.

The path leads out of the forest and up a rocky hill.

You come to the top of a ridge, looking down over a flat, grassy area with a wooden building that must be the ranger's hut. A strange futuristic aircraft sits on the grass, sort of like a jet, but standing on its wings, which are folded down by its side as if they were legs.

"What in the world is that?" you wonder.

Carmen snaps a picture and sends it to Player. He tells her that he's not sure, but it looks like a helijet, an experimental aircraft that can fly like a jet and hover like a helicopter.

"I don't think that belongs to the park rangers," you say.

"VILE tech for sure," says Carmen. "Someone's coming!"

A Japanese woman wearing a kimono and carrying a parasol comes out of the hut. She is flanked by three VILE guards in black suits, one of them carrying a satchel that you guess must hold the kakapo egg.

"That's Lady Dokuso," Carmen whispers. "One of VILE's best operatives. *Dokuso* is the Japanese word for toxin or poison."

You don't like the sound of that. Carmen's face shows intense focus as she studies the situation. "I'd rather not take them on directly," she says, "but with so little time, I don't have a choice. I'll handle the VILE guards. You look for a chance to grab that egg."

Carmen sprints toward Lady Dokuso and the VILE guards, then leaps into the air. Suddenly, a red hang glider springs out from her back and she takes flight. She soars down the hill, kicking the guard with the satchel from behind.

The guard tumbles to the ground, dropping the satchel. The two remaining guards wheel to face Carmen, while Lady Dokuso dashes up the heli-jet stairs. You run down the hill, ready to grab the satchel or join the fight.

And then Lady Dokuso raises her para-sol and aims it toward Carmen. *What is she doing?* A dart shoots from the tip of the para-sol—but Carmen grabs one of the guards and swings him around in front of her so that the dart hits the guard instead. He immediately falls unconscious.

Lady Dokuso pulls something out of her hair and flings it at the ground. The thing bursts into a cloud of purple smoke that sur-rounds Carmen and all three guards. You almost run into the smoke yourself but stop short just in time.

Carmen staggers and then collapses in a

heap. The smoke must be some sort of knockout poison! The guards that Carmen was fighting fall too—Lady Dokuso didn't care if she knocked out her own people so long as she got Carmen.

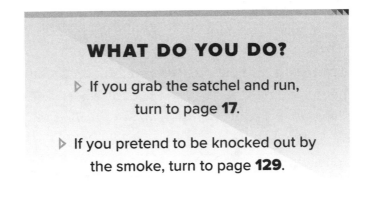

WHAT DO YOU DO?

▷ If you grab the satchel and run, turn to page **17**.

▷ If you pretend to be knocked out by the smoke, turn to page **129**.

YOU RUSH OUT of the bridge and down the stairs to intercept Otter Man.

"What's going on?" he snaps at you. "I think we're slowing down."

"The captain says we're having mechanical trouble," you tell him. "He says he should have it fixed in a couple of minutes."

"Mechanical trouble? The engines are still on; they're just in reverse." He pushes past you. "I'm going to talk to the captain."

"Tell him there's a whale," Player suggests in your ear.

"Wait—it's actually a whale," you insist. "We were going to hit a whale, so we had to slow down."

Otter Man just waves you off. "A whale? That makes zero sense. Anyway, we don't exactly care about endangered animals on this ship."

"Sorry," says Player. *"It was the best I could think of on short notice."*

Otter Man is up the stairs now and onto the bridge. You see him talking to the captain, who is pointing at you. *Uh-oh.* Now Otter Man is talking to someone on his phone. You decide this would be a good time to get out of sight, so you head for the stairs that lead below deck, when a powerful hand grabs you from behind.

"You seemed so nice," says Moose Boy as he lifts you by the back of the shirt. "I'm sorry you turned out to be a traitor."

With a massive heave, he hurls you through the air and over the railing at the side of the ship. You plunge down into the cold, salty water, going under for a few seconds and then popping back to the surface. The ship looms massively overhead and you swim away from it, not wanting to be caught up in the pull of the engines.

"Player," you say, "are you there?" But the water seems to have shorted out the earpiece, and there's no reply.

You are clear of the ship now, swimming as hard as you can. But you have no idea how far you are from shore, and honestly, your chances don't seem good.

THE END

YOU SIP YOUR PINEAPPLE JUICE,

watching Le Chèvre as he watches a video on his tablet. Ten minutes later, El Topo comes back to the table. "My friend," he says, "let us return to our search. There is a lot of jungle out there and only one little snake."

Le Chèvre agrees. The two men walk right past the table where you are sitting, while you are careful not to make eye contact. You wish again that Carmen were here, but she's not, and you know that you can't let these two criminals disappear. You count to ten and then follow them out onto the road.

The two men get into a green pickup truck about a hundred feet away. As Le Chèvre slams his door, you dash toward them, keeping your head low. Just as the truck starts to move, you hoist yourself into the cargo bed in the back and duck down.

They don't see you. It's probably the sneakiest thing you've ever done.

They drive out of the village along a road that leads deeper into the forest, with you as their unknown passenger. There is a large bucket next to you in the cargo bed, as well as a snake hook—supplies to catch and transport the Cropan's boa.

Le Chèvre drives while El Topo holds the tracker up in the air, adjusting a dial, trying to pick up the snake's signal. They are talking, but you can't hear what they are saying from your hiding place in the back.

Finally, after an hour of driving along bumpy roads, Le Chèvre stops the truck. El Topo opens his door and steps out. You realize that he will probably come to the back to get his supplies, so you climb out of the cargo bed. The forest is thick here, so you dive into the bushes and crouch low, peeking out between the leaves.

El Topo holds the tracker in the air, listens to it, turns the dial, and then gets back into the truck. To your surprise, Le Chèvre starts driving again and the pickup truck rumbles away, too fast for you to climb back in.

You realize that you have been left behind, somewhere deep in the Atlantic Forest, with no way to get back to civilization. You have no food or water. It's already late afternoon.

With no other choice, you start walking down the road the way you came. You think you will make it back eventually, but by then, Carmen's crew and VILE will probably both be long gone.

THE END

"LET'S WAIT FOR VILE," you say. "If we follow them, we might find out where they're keeping all the stolen animals."

"Just what I was thinking," Carmen agrees.

There's nothing to do now except wait. The car gets hot and stuffy as the afternoon drags on. You get out for some fresh air, peering into the dense growth of the Atlantic Forest. You imagine the Cropan's boa hanging around somewhere in all that green.

"Hey!" Ivy shouts. "The beeping is getting faster. We're not moving, so that means the snake is coming toward us!"

"VILE must have found the snake!" Carmen says. "They'll take her somewhere for a handoff. We should hide and let them pass, and then follow them to find the rest of the animals."

The four of you push into the forest, ducking behind the bushes that grow alongside the road. The beeping gets faster until you see a green pickup truck drive past. "The transmitter is on that truck," Ivy says in an excited whisper, "which means the snake is on that truck."

Once the truck is out of sight, the four of you get

back into your car. "Stay on their tail," Carmen tells Zack. "Let's find out where they're going."

Zack pulls out and follows the truck. "Not a problem, boss." After a few miles, the road opens onto a straightaway with farmland on either side. You can see the green pickup truck ahead.

"Not too close," Carmen warns. "Don't let them see that they're being followed."

Zack lets the pickup truck get farther ahead. It's often out of sight, but as long as the tracker keeps beeping, you know you are close. You seem to be heading south, farther away from São Paulo.

"Hold on; slow down," Ivy says. She holds up her tracker, and you hear that the beeping has gotten slower.

"They must have turned off the road somewhere," Carmen says. "Zack, turn around."

When you head back in the other direction, you notice a very rough road that branches off from the main one, little more than a path through the forest where the trees have been cleared away. The beeping is very quick now, which means that the snake—and VILE—are close.

Zack stops the car, and Carmen gets out. "On foot from here," she says. "I don't want anyone to hear us coming."

The four of you creep through the forest, the beeps still getting faster. Up ahead, you see sunlight where the path opens into a clearing. You take a few more steps and see a large field, with the pickup truck that you have been following parked on one side. There is a large bucket in the truck's cargo bed, which must contain the snake. Two men stand nearby talking, one tall and wiry, the other short and strong.

"Le Chèvre and El Topo," Carmen whispers. "VILE operatives."

"What are they doing?" Ivy wonders.

In the distance, you hear the drone of an engine, slowly getting louder. Looking up, you see the silhouette of an airplane coming in for a landing on the field. "They're making the handoff," Carmen realizes.

The plane gets lower and then touches down, rumbling across the field and coming to a stop close to Le Chèvre and El Topo. A door opens from the cockpit, and a pilot leans out. "Here for the pickup," she says.

"Greetings," says El Topo. "How was your flight?"

"Good enough," the pilot says. "I just came from Kansas, picking up some ferret thing. You're my last stop before the final drop-off."

"The package is ready," says Le Chèvre. "Please open the cargo hold."

The pilot goes back inside the cockpit, and a few seconds later, a hatch opens in the middle of the plane with the whir of a hydraulic motor.

"I need to sneak onto that plane," Carmen says. "It will take me wherever VILE is keeping the rest of the stolen animals. There's only one door, though, and I don't think I can get past Le Chèvre and El Topo in broad daylight, unless . . ."

" . . . unless we create a distraction," Ivy finishes the thought.

"Distraction is my middle name," Zack adds proudly. "Watch this!"

Zack hollers and charges out into the field, directly toward El Topo and Le Chèvre. "Maybe not the best plan," Ivy says, "but I guess we're going with it." She charges out into the field too, about thirty feet behind her brother.

El Topo throws himself toward the ground and begins to dig like a mole, disappearing into the dirt. Le Chèvre goes into a fighting stance and, a moment before Zack reaches him, leaps up to grab the airplane wing with both hands. He somersaults into the air and comes down right on top of Zack, pinning him to the ground with his knees. "You!" he sneers. "What are you doing here?"

"Get your filthy knees off my brother!" Ivy shouts, charging toward Le Chèvre. Suddenly, the earth opens beneath her feet and El Topo pops out, tackling her from behind by the ankles. She crashes to the ground.

You run for the pickup truck that Le Chèvre and El Topo were driving. Seeing that the key is still in the ignition, you slide into the driver's seat and gun the engine, speeding toward the fight. When Le Chèvre sees the truck barreling toward him, he releases Zack and vaults up on top of the airplane wing. El Topo dives and burrows back into the ground.

You turn the steering wheel hard and slam the brakes a moment before you run into Zack and Ivy. "Get in!" you shout. The two of them grab ahold of the back of the truck, climbing into the cargo bed as you speed away. Out of the corner of your eye, you see Carmen slipping through the open hatch into the airplane's cargo hold.

Le Chèvre and El Topo sprint behind you, but they have no chance of catching the truck. You careen down the path through the forest until you reach the main road. Zack and Ivy get back into their car, and the three of you race away.

After driving for a while, you all stop by the side of the road to check on the snake and make a plan. You lift the lid off the bucket to find a heavy cloth sack inside. Peeking inside the sack, you see a coil of yellow-and-black scales in a diamond pattern.

"Whoa," says Ivy. "We should let her go."

You look around at the forest. "We need to leave her where VILE can't find her again. The range on the tracker is pretty short, so if we drop her somewhere a hundred miles away, they won't even know where to start looking."

You decide that Zack and Ivy should drive their car back to São Paulo, while you drive the boa into the forest to find a good place to release her. The sun has gone down now, and you drive on your own along dark roads deeper into the forest.

There's a device with a video screen on the dashboard of the VILE truck, attached by a suction cup. You assumed it was a GPS—but suddenly it flashes on, showing a large woman with a fierce scowl on her face. "I don't know who I'm talking to," she says, "but you're driving my property."

At first, you're too surprised to answer. Can she see you somehow through the screen?

"You're Carmen's little friend, right?" the woman seethes. "Well, sugar, you tangled with the wrong people today. How about you bring me my snake back and we'll forget this ever happened?"

"Not a chance," you say, looking for an OFF button on the device.

"Hold on!" the woman says. "Actually, this might be your lucky day. You see, I'm collecting a whole zoo full of animals, and that snake you're hauling is one of the last I need. That makes it valuable to me. *Very* valuable. So, tell me, what kind of money do you like wherever you're from?"

"Euros," you say.

"Okay, sure. I'm about to ping you a destination. All you need to do is park that truck where I tell you and walk away, and I'll pay you a hundred thousand euros for your trouble."

"I would never—"

"I don't have time to negotiate. Let's make it two hundred thousand euros. Imagine how many endangered animals you could help with that kind of money. I promise we'll give your scaly friend a good home, with a nice tree to climb and plenty of freeze-dried mice to eat."

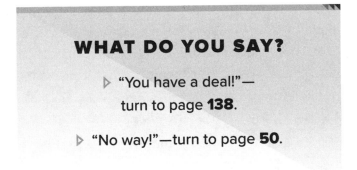

WHAT DO YOU SAY?

▷ "You have a deal!"—
turn to page **138**.

▷ "No way!"—turn to page **50**.

YOU HAVE A FEELING that Tigress is someone you should avoid, so you stick to your hiding spot, crouching low in the bushes until she is gone.

A few minutes later, you hear a ***WHOOSH,*** and Carmen drops out of the air onto the path next to you. She looks frustrated. "I almost caught up with the van," she says. "But they slipped away this time."

"There was someone else here," you tell her. "Someone named Tigress."

"Of course." Carmen frowns. "It figures they sent Tigress to steal a tiger."

"You know her?"

"We were friends once—well, not friends, exactly. Anyway, we've tangled a few times, but it looks like this time she got away."

"I'm sorry," you say. "I should have tried to stop her."

Carmen shakes her head. "Tigress is dangerous, and you were smart to stay away from her." Seeing your disappointed face, she puts a hand on your shoulder. "Look," she says, "in the real world, sometimes the bad guys win. It's not your fault."

But you can't help feeling that it's a little bit your fault.

DESPITE IVY'S CONFIDENCE, you decide that the safest thing is to get rid of the tracker, and so you pitch it over the side of the boat, where it sinks under the waves.

"Suit yourself," says Ivy as Zack pushes the throttle and speeds toward shore.

Within a few hours, the three of you have docked at a marina on the mainland. You hear from Player that Carmen managed to land the helicopter and will meet you there soon. Zack and Ivy have gone into a diner to get some takeout, while you sit on a bench outside, watching boats come and go.

You are holding on to Carmen's red fedora until you can return it to her. You try it on your head and find that it fits well. *So this is what it feels like to be the world's greatest thief,* you think with a smile.

Suddenly, a green van screeches to a stop on the street in front of you, and the back door flies open. You glimpse a woman in a kimono aiming her parasol at you—and then you feel a sting in your neck. You touch the spot and pull out a tiny dart as the world goes fuzzy. The last thing you hear before you lose consciousness is someone saying, "That's not Carmen Sandiego!"

When you come to, you are lying on a tangle of vines next to a hollow tree trunk. Where in the world are you? Looking around, you realize that you are inside an animal enclosure like the kind you have in a zoo, with a mesh wire fence on all sides.

Outside the enclosure, you see the woman in the kimono, the one who shot you with the poison dart, talking to a much larger woman. "Good job getting the kakapo, Lady D," the large woman says. "But why did you bring back that zookeeper?"

"I apologize, Coach Brunt. We thought we were capturing Carmen Sandiego."

Coach Brunt peers in at you. "A minor mistake in an otherwise outstanding mission," she says. "We'll get this cleaned up in no time."

When the two women leave, you try to get out of the enclosure, but you can't break the fence, and the gate is locked from the outside. You have no choice but to wait to be "cleaned up"—whatever that means.

THE END

YOU DECIDE TO STAY with Nadezhda, even if it means putting yourself in danger.

Tigress does a running handspring, vaulting up into the air and incredibly landing on top of the fence around the zoo. All the guards' flashlights focus on her as she holds her hands up in the air. "Catch me if you can," she taunts, and then does an acrobatic flip off the fence and back inside the zoo.

The guards shout and chase her as she sprints away down the dark path. "Hmm," says Otter Man. "It appears that Tigress has distracted the guards, *ja*? Now we make our escape."

You ride in the back of the van with Nadezhda while Otter Man drives and Moose Boy rides in the front passenger seat. There's a bottle of formula in a pocket on the outside of the carrying case, and you offer it to the baby tiger, making shushing sounds to calm her down. It seems to be working as she settles onto her blanket and starts chomping on the nipple, sending squirts of the nutritious liquid into her mouth.

In the front of the van, a video screen on the dashboard blinks on to show a large Texan woman with a huge smile on her face. "Howdy, animal wranglers. Tigress tells me you got another one."

"*Ja,* Coach Brunt," says Otter Man. "Another successful mission under my leadership."

From the video screen, Coach Brunt peers past the two operatives and into the back of the van. "Looks like you picked up a human passenger too," she says.

"That is correct," Otter Man explains nervously. "Tigress thought this zookeeper might help with the animals."

Brunt considers you. "Hmm . . . . You like animals, sugar?"

That's an easy question. "I do like them," you say, "but for me, it's more about *respect,* giving every animal the chance to live a full and dignified life."

Brunt smiles warmly. "Aw, you're tugging this mama bear's heartstrings. I hereby declare you the official zookeeper of VILE."

"Um, wh-what's VILE?"

"Now, don't you worry about that, sugar. Brunt out." The video screen flashes to black.

As the van bumps along through the night, you find yourself getting sleepy, despite everything. You lean your head against the wall, thinking you'll just rest your eyes . . . and you wake up hours later to the sound of seagulls and the smell of the ocean. "Where are we?" you ask sleepily.

"Trieste," Otter Man replies coldly.

You know that Trieste is a major port city on the Adriatic Sea, at the northern tip of Italy, which means you've driven all the way through Slovenia. It also means that you are probably getting on a ship.

Sure enough, the van drives onto a long dock where a cargo ship is tied up to one side. A gangplank leads down from the ship to the dock. "Our ride is here," says Otter Man dryly. "Moose, unload the kitty. Zookeeper, get on board and stay out of trouble."

You walk up the gangplank. The crew ignores you as they go about their business. As you look around, you realize that this ship has been converted into a sort of floating zoo! There are four large crates on deck to hold the animals, each with one wall made of clear plexiglass with holes for breathing.

You investigate the largest crate and find a black rhino, chomping mouthfuls of hay. The next two hold a giant panda and a bonobo, a rare primate that lives near the Congo River in Africa and resembles a chimpanzee.

You feel a pang of frustration that these animals don't have as much room as they should to move around, but you figure it's only temporary until they get wherever they're going. Moose Boy unloads Nadezhda into the final crate. You're relieved to see that the inside has things for her to climb and places for her to hide.

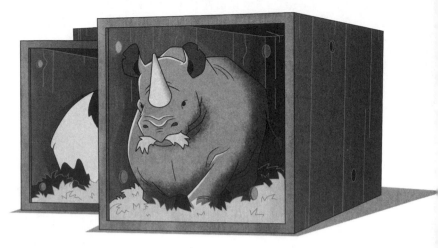

When the ship starts moving, most of the crew disappears below deck. "It's all going to be okay," you tell Nadezhda, and then notice that she has curled up and fallen asleep. Maybe you should do the same.

You hear a faint buzzing behind you and turn around to see— *What in the world is that?*

Right behind you, a round metal ball floats in the air, with a big camera eye that seems to be looking at you. The thing bobs up and down, left and right, as if considering you from different angles. You realize that it must be a drone, but who's controlling it?

A small hatch opens on the bottom of the drone, and something drops out onto the deck of the ship with a light clang. You pick the thing up and see that it's an electronic device with a handwritten note attached to it.

Put me in your ear.

Here, on the strangest night of your life, may be the strangest thing yet. You're not really going to put a mysterious device inside your ear. Are you?

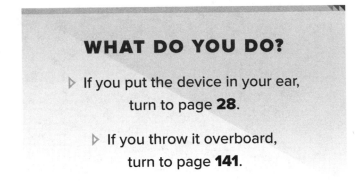

WHAT DO YOU DO?

▷ If you put the device in your ear,
turn to page **28**.

▷ If you throw it overboard,
turn to page **141**.

You sway dramatically on your feet
and then fall to the ground as if you had breathed in
the poison smoke. You hope your performance is con-
vincing.

Lady Dokuso stands at the entryway to the helijet,
looking down at the five unconscious bodies scattered
on the ground in the moonlight. "Why must I do everything?" she mutters to herself.

She walks down the stairway and crouches behind
one of the unconscious guards, clasping her hands
across the guard's chest. With a grunt of effort, she
drags the guard across the grass and up the stairs into
the helijet.

Lady Dokuso comes next for the other two guards
and then for Carmen. Finally, she comes for you, wrapping her arms around you and pulling you from behind.
Your feet bump painfully up the helijet stairs, but you
manage to stay perfectly limp the whole time.

The cabin inside the helijet is a single room, with
benches bolted to either wall. Carmen lies flopped on
one of the benches. Lady Dokuso has propped the
guards up against the back wall, as if they were sitting

three in a row. She heaves you onto the other bench, breathing heavily from the effort.

At the front of the cabin is the helijet's cockpit, with a complicated-looking flight computer. The cabin door swings shut as Lady Dokuso starts pressing buttons, and then you feel a lurch in your stomach as thrusters come online and the helijet shoots straight up into the air.

Lady Dokuso leans back in her chair, taking a moment to relax. *I have only one chance at this,* you think. *I need to choose the perfect moment to strike.* You know that she's a trained VILE operative and you are a regular person, so your only advantage is surprise.

When Lady Dokuso comes into the back of the cabin, you lie perfectly still on your bench, trying not to even breathe. She stands over Carmen, poking with the tip of her parasol to make sure that the young thief is still unconscious. "Such a shame," Dokuso says to Carmen. "You could have been one of VILE's best."

Now. You leap from your bench and charge into Lady Dokuso's back, knocking her against the opposite wall and sending her parasol skittering across the floor. You charge a second time, but she steps nimbly out of the way and uses your momentum to throw you down onto the pile of unconscious guards.

"Well, well," she says. "Look who woke up early."

Lady Dokuso stalks toward you. Desperately, you pick up her parasol, thinking that you can use it to defend yourself. The parasol pops open in front of you, and you hear a **WHOOSH,** followed by a **THUNK.**

Peeking over the rim of the parasol, you see Lady Dokuso lying unconscious on the floor! You must have accidentally triggered the poison dart!

What now? You find some rope in a storage bin and tie up Lady Dokuso and each of the guards as best as you can — and then to be sure, you hit each one with an extra knockout dart from the parasol. You have no idea where the jet is going but decide not to touch the controls.

Thirty minutes later, you see that Carmen is stirring. She rubs her eyes and sits up woozily. "What happened?" she asks. You tell her everything. "Nice work," she says with a smile.

Carmen staggers to her feet, still unsteady from the

poison, and collapses into the cockpit chair. She takes a device out of her coat and plugs it into a port on the computer. "Player," she says, "I just plugged into the helijet's navigation system. Can you get in?"

Player's face appears on a monitor above the computer. *"Good to hear from you, Red. You went dark for a while there."*

"You have no idea," Carmen says.

"And . . . I'm in," says Player. *"It looks like the VILE helijet has a sophisticated autopilot, no humans required. Right now, you're headed for an island off the coast of Greece. That must be where they're taking all the animals."*

"We'll deal with that later," Carmen says. "For now, let's set a new course. First stop, Paris. I have some passengers I want to drop off with Interpol."

"And where to after that?" Player asks.

"Not sure," says Carmen, "but I'm pretty sure that having our own self-flying jet will come in handy, wouldn't you say?"

"Copy that," says Player, and the monitor blinks off.

"What about you?" Carmen asks. "I'm happy to drop you back in Vienna. But what you did today was amazing, and I'm thinking I could use someone like you as a permanent part of my crew."

WHAT DO YOU DO?

▷ If you go back to zookeeping,
   turn to page **91**.

▷ If you join Carmen's crew,
   turn to page **145**.

YOU DECIDE THAT your best chance is to swim for safety. You guess you're at least a mile from Stewart Island and even farther from the mainland — too far to swim, especially since ocean currents can be unpredictable. You spot a tiny island nearby, just a mound of rock big enough for a single lonely tree. You swim in that direction.

As you fight the waves, you worry that you will be swept past the island. You kick off your shoes to swim more easily and push as hard as you can, a sense of panic growing in your chest. Desperately, you reach out and grab a point of rock, pulling yourself onto land.

Dripping wet, you sit on a rock to catch your breath. You're safe, at least for the moment. In the distance, you see two boats racing across the ocean, spraying water behind them, but they're so far away now that you can't tell which one is Carmen's.

You suddenly feel very alone, on a tiny island in an unfamiliar ocean. You have nothing to eat or drink. Sure, Carmen and her crew know where you are in general, but will they be able to come back this way with Interpol watching? And even if they do, will they be able to find you?

After a couple of fretful hours, you see a ship coming toward you. It's the Interpol cruiser, the one that started chasing you in the first place. Under the circumstances, you decide you're better off letting them know you're here. You stand at the edge of the tiny island, waving your arms. The cruiser turns toward you.

As it approaches, you see Chase Devineaux standing on deck, grinning proudly. He orders the cruiser close to where you are standing and then tosses a rope ladder down the side. "We saw you jump from Carmen Sandiego's boat," he shouts, "and came to rescue you. Come, swim to me. I am eager to speak with you."

Reluctantly, you dive back into the water and swim with tired arms to the Interpol cruiser. You catch the rope ladder and haul yourself up until you stand wearily on the deck.

"Take our guest inside," Chase barks. "We have much to discuss."

Two Interpol officers grab you roughly and take you inside the cabin of the cruiser. To your dismay, they sit you on a bench and handcuff your wrists behind you—treating you like their prisoner.

A few minutes later, Chase comes into the cabin and sits across from you. "Well, well. Carmen Sandiego may have slipped through my fingers once again, but it seems I have captured one of her associates, *oui*?"

You start to speak, but he interrupts you. "No! I will

ask the questions here. Tell me, why is Carmen Sandiego stealing exotic animals from all around the world? A rhinoceros from Kenya. A red wolf from North Carolina. A tiger cub from Vienna. And now I receive a tip that someone is trying to steal one of the chubby parrots from here in New Zealand."

"Inspector Devineaux," you protest, "you have it backwards. Carmen is trying to *save* the animals. I know. I work at the zoo in Vienna where the Amur tiger cub was stolen."

"Aha," says Chase confidently. "I knew it was an inside job!"

"No, that's not what I said. It was . . . a criminal organization called VILE, some of the most dangerous criminals in the world."

Chase leans in close. "Enough lies. Tell me now where I can find Carmen Sandiego, or I will hold you personally responsible for every single animal theft."

"I don't know," you say. You really don't know where Carmen is now, and even if you did, you wouldn't tell Chase Devineaux.

When you arrive back on land,

you are immediately arrested and taken into custody by Interpol. Chase says that you will be going to prison for a very long time. You know you are innocent, but your story is so strange, you fear that no one will believe you.

"YOU HAVE A DEAL!" you say.

The woman smiles and tells you that half of the money has already been transferred into your bank account. The other half will come as soon as she gets her snake back. You check your account on your phone and see that you are indeed one hundred thousand euros richer!

The woman's face disappears from the screen and is replaced by a map, with a flashing ping at a nearby location. You turn the truck around and head for the marked spot, which turns out to be a bus station. As instructed, you park the pickup truck and catch the next bus for São Paulo.

Two days later, you are back home in Vienna. The whole crazy adventure seems like a dream—but the mountain of money in your bank account is very real. You give most of it to charities that help save endangered species around the world but save enough to buy yourself a sweet new car. You figure that you've earned it.

THE END

"NO," YOU SAY. "I don't want to be a thief, and besides, if I'm being honest, I really hate how you've been stealing all these animals."

"Well, I'm sorry to hear that," says Brunt, and then pulls out her phone. "Brunt here. I'm going to need the Cleaners down at the docks ASAP."

The Cleaners? You don't like the sound of that.

"Maybe we can compromise," you say. "Just take me back to Vienna, drop me at the Schönbrunn Zoo, and I promise not to cause any trouble or mention anything to anyone about any of this."

"Sorry, sugar, but that horse has left the barn. You made your decision, and now I'm going to need you to park yourself on that bench over there until some friends of mine arrive."

You do as she says. What choice do you have? A few minutes later, two men wearing janitor uniforms, one short and one tall, emerge from the large gray building. They walk over and stand right in front of you.

"Greetings," says the short one in a Russian accent. "You will be coming with us now, I think." The two men grab you, one on each arm, their grips painfully strong. They stand you up and lead you back toward the building.

"Where are you taking me?" you ask.

"No conversations, please," the tall one responds.

As the doors to VILE Academy slide open and the Cleaners lead you inside, you have a feeling that this is . . .

THE END

YOU'RE NOT ABOUT to put some random gizmo into your ear. You pitch the device over the railing and into the ocean. The red drone considers you for another moment and then buzzes away.

You decide that this night has been strange enough and that maybe you should get some rest, so you go below deck. Finding a small cabin with a cot inside, you stretch out and go to sleep. When you wake up and come back out on deck, it's a beautiful morning, the sun sparkling over the Mediterranean Sea.

Moose Boy stands at the ship's railing, so you walk over to join him. "Where are we going?" you ask.

"I'm not supposed to tell you anything," he says cautiously, "so let's just say that it's a private island with its own secret zoo off the coast of Greece." He slaps himself on the forehead. "I guess I just told you a lot."

You pat him on the shoulder. "That's okay. It will be our secret."

Sure enough, within a few hours, you are approaching a green jewel of an island that rises out of the Mediterranean. You know that Greece has thousands of islands and that if you have enough money, it's possible to buy one all for yourself.

The cargo ship sails into a natural harbor where the crew ties up at a long dock. A crane attached to the dock lifts the first animal crate, the one with the giant panda, off the ship and onto a waiting flatbed truck. Once the crate is secure, the truck drives away on a road that leads over a ridge.

No one seems to be paying any attention to you, so you decide to follow the truck. When you reach the top of the ridge, you are astonished to see an entire zoo. There are a few carefully constructed habitats separated by fences. In one rocky enclosure, a Komodo dragon suns itself on a rock. There's even a large water tank, where you glimpse a sea turtle swimming around.

Near the entrance to the zoo, Coach Brunt is talking to a man in a perfect tan suit. "The master is pleased," the man says. "However, we cannot send payment until the three final animals are delivered."

"Fair enough," says Brunt. "They'll be here soon. In the meantime, I'm happy to stay and enjoy your Greek hospitality. How about someone fixes me a gyro?" Brunt notices you. "Plus," she says to the man in the suit, "I got you a bonus. We're throwing in a free zookeeper, from a fancy zoo in Vienna." She waves for you to come over. "Zookeeper, come on and introduce yourself!"

You shake the man's hand. "I do have to get back home eventually," you say nervously, "but I'm happy to help the animals get settled."

Brunt frowns at you. "Now, now, sugar, I thought you understood. When you take a job with VILE, it's a permanent position."

"Wait . . . you mean I'm supposed to stay here . . . forever?"

"That's what *permanent* means." Coach Brunt clenches her fists in a way that tells you not to argue anymore. "You're a zookeeper," she says. "Now, go do some zookeeping!"

The next day, two more animals arrive by cargo plane, a black-footed ferret and a Cropan's boa from the Americas. All the animals are put into their new habitats and start to settle in. Finally, a kakapo egg is delivered from New Zealand, which you'll need to watch carefully until it hatches. With the zoo complete, Coach Brunt takes her payment and leaves.

As weeks and months go by, you get used to your new life. You are made the head zookeeper, with two assistants to help you. The zoo is mostly well designed, but you do have ideas to improve some of the animals' homes. The man in the tan suit tells you that he can get anything you need, and sure enough, everything you ask for arrives by boat within days. You meet some of the other staff on the island: an army of gardeners, grounds-keepers, cooks, carpenters, and cleaners. Some of them become your friends.

Every so often, the master of the island throws a party that includes a tour of the private zoo. His guests *ooh* and *aah* while he talks about how incredibly rare the animals are and what a privilege it is to see them.

Months stretch into years, and Nadezhda is now a strong and beautiful Amur tiger. It's certainly not the life you expected—head zookeeper at an illegal zoo on a private Greek island—but it's not a bad life . . . not really.

THE END

"YES," YOU TELL CARMEN. "I'll join your crew."

"Perfect," she says.

Carmen drops Lady Dokuso and her team, still unconscious, in a park outside Paris. She calls Interpol with an anonymous tip to pick them up, saying that they are responsible for all the animal thefts. She also tells Interpol that the stolen animals can be found on an island off the coast of Greece.

From there, you start your new life with Carmen's crew. She teaches you thieving skills, like self-defense, sneaking, deactivating security systems, picking locks, and picking pockets. You travel with Carmen all around the world, using your new talents to stop VILE's schemes.

Before long, she trusts you to handle capers on your own. You break into the Metropolitan Museum of Art, a top-secret tech lab in Munich, and a bank vault in Singapore. You never imagined that you would become a thief, but it turns out that you're a great one — fast, smart, and stealthy.

Like Carmen, you steal only for good, never for

personal profit. You are proud to be part of Carmen Sandiego's crew and grateful to be her friend.

THE END

Create more exciting adventures
with **CARMEN SANDIEGO**
when you *chase your own caper*
in

Turn the page for a sneak peak!

VILE PLOT

THE FIVE VILE INSTRUCTORS were gathered in the faculty lounge, discussing their latest defeat at the hands of Carmen Sandiego.

Coach Brunt, an enormously strong Texan who taught self-defense, shook her head sadly. "Black Sheep could have been VILE's best operative, then she had to go and betray her family. Sometimes I wonder where I went wrong."

"Let's not dwell in the past," snapped Professor Maelstrom, a gaunt man with a wicked face. "Black Sheep no longer exists. Now she is Carmen Sandiego, our sworn enemy, and she must be stopped *by any means necessary.*"

"It will not be easy," grumbled Shadowsan, a grim Japanese man trained as a ninja. "Carmen Sandiego is fast, she is strong, and, most of all, she is smart."

"She also had the worst table manners of any student I can remember," said Countess Cleo, with her nose in the air. "To be honest, I never thought she'd amount to anything."

The fifth VILE instructor, Dr. Saira Bellum, wasn't paying attention to the conversation. She had five computer monitors open in front of her, tapping away at one with her left hand and another with her right hand, while looking at a third.

"Dr. Bellum," said Maelstrom wearily, "do *you* have anything to contribute?"

Bellum's specialty was science and gadgetry. "Oh, indeed I do," she said with a mad chuckle. "Perhaps our operatives will not be so worried about Carmen Sandiego—*once they are able to fly.*"

The four other instructors stared at Bellum blankly, waiting for her to explain.

"Jetpacks!" she exclaimed, waving her hands in the air. "Ten months ago, I hired a top technology company to build them according to my plans. The first jetpacks will be delivered tomorrow. Just imagine, VILE operatives will be able to strike from the sky at any time!"

"Well," said Countess Cleo with a sly smile, "I have always enjoyed looking down on people."

"Excellent," Maelstrom agreed. "It seems that we have some good news today after all."

Will VILE succeed in their plot to become flying criminals? In this story, it's up to you. Your choices will lead to one of twenty endings.

ARE YOU READY?

Turn the page.

YOU ARE AN ENGINEER at Zeta Circuits, a technology company in Singapore.

You have lived your whole life in Singapore, a city at the southern tip of the Malay Peninsula in Asia. Long ago, the area belonged to fishermen and pirates, and later became part of a British colony. Today Singapore is its own country—your grandparents remember when it declared independence in 1965.

As one of the busiest ports in the world and a hub of high-tech manufacturing, Singapore is bursting with

opportunities for a smart engineer like you. In fact, you recently got the chance of a lifetime: a job on a top-secret project for Zeta Circuits.

You have been working on personal jetpacks, small enough to wear on your back, powerful enough to let a human fly like a bird. Although you are part of a large team, you have made important contributions, especially to the design of the rockets. After ten months of hard work, the jetpacks are finished.

Tonight you are working late, reviewing the results from the final flight tests—but after sixteen hours of staring at numbers on your computer screen, you have dozed off at your desk. You wake up

disoriented, looking around your dimly lit office. All your coworkers are gone. Glancing at the clock on your computer, you see that it is 2:30 in the morning.

On the other side of the room, the door to the vault that holds the jetpacks is cracked open. *That's strange.* The vault has a thick metal door, which can only be unlocked by a fingerprint sensor. It's always supposed to be closed, to guard against